TALES FROM THE SILVER STATE IV

Tales from the Silver State IV

TALES FROM THE SILVER STATE IV

Short Fiction by members of the Las Vegas Writers' Group.

The Authors:

- Noëlle de Beaufort
- Tina Contini
- Jay Hill
- John Hill
- Susan Joslyn
- Danét Palmer
- Marshall Prescott
- Edward Riepe
- Susanne Rowe
- Thom Slaughter
- Tonya Todd
- Virginia Vennare

Tales from the Silver State IV

Compiled by Steven Fey, these stories are presented unedited, as fresh and original as when they were first written down.

These stories are works of fiction. Names, places, characters, and incidents are the products of the respective author's imagination, or are used fictionally. Any resemblance to actual places, events, or persons living or dead, is purely coincidental.

ISBN-13: 978-0-9989720-0-8

ISBN-10: 0-9989720-0-2

E-book ISBN: 978-0-9989720-1-5

Printed in the United States of America

TheFeyCow, Las Vegas, Nevada

Tales from the Silver State IV *is set in Palatino Linotype, an oldstyle font noted for being easy to read, and used in many books.*

Tales from the Silver State IV

THE STORIES ARE PRESENTED ALPHABETICALLY BY AUTHOR'S LAST NAME

Tales from the Silver State IV *is set in Palatino Linotype, an oldstyle font noted for being easy to read, and used in many books.*

Tales from the Silver State IV

THE PRICE OF LUCK

By Tina Contini

Silent prayers floated like dying embers upon the breeze. A slender man with dark circles under his hopeful eyes rubbed a smooth quarter between his fingers and rolled it across his knuckles. The sound of money filled the casino, and even from the hotel registration, he could hear the clang of coins dropping into the slot baskets. He closed his eyes and added his spark to the fire. *Please, send luck my way.* The quarter moved faster back and forth as he inched his way to the front.

"Good evening, Sir. How may I help you?"

He glanced at the girl, barely noticing how attractive she was. "Checking in. John Rodgers."

Her pink, shiny show lips curved into a perfect smile. "Just a moment." She tucked a strand of her feathered hair behind her ear and started typing.

He turned and looked into the casino. Massive chandeliers glittered over a sea of plush carpeting. John tucked his lucky coin into the top pocket of his jacket and patted it for luck.

"All set, Sir. You have a lovely room on the 24th floor." She handed him the room key, her manicured nails matched her rose lip gloss. "Good luck and have a Grand stay with us."

John snatched the key and grabbed his duffel bag. Mumbling thanks, he turned to what attracted him. She was beautiful, every machine and table singing to him like a Siren. He struggled to his room reminding himself he had three days and two nights to answer the call.

Time was valuable and instead of admiring the shimmering lights of Las Vegas Blvd, John tossed his duffel bag on the king sized bed, took out his wallet, and pulled out the last of his bank account. He counted the crisp bills and placed them into three piles on the bed. The first stack went back into his wallet, and he looked around the room for the first time. It was larger than the studio apartment he now rented by the week. The other two piles were folded in half; one tucked deep into the pillow on the bed and the other under a chair cushion. Patting his pockets to make sure he had the room key and wallet, he left without a second glance.

John stopped pacing and pressed the elevator button a third time. When it opened, laughter filled the empty corridor. He shoved past the young couple and as the elevator took him down, memories of his first trip to Vegas filled his thoughts. He told himself he wanted to propose to Gloria and get married without all the fuss and expense of a wedding, but was that true? Even all those years ago, did he love gambling more than her?

He traded his money for chips, a smaller stack than what he anticipated, and circled the 21 tables. Each time around his pace quickened, and his lucky coin rolled across his knuckles faster. Finally, a beaten down man left, and John grabbed the spot. He had seen that same face looking back at himself in the mirror too many times.

Lady Luck did not grace him tonight, and he was back in his room in less than an hour. John plopped down on the bed and lit his first cigarette. Numerous times his hand felt inside the cool pillow case and touched the money set aside for tomorrow's gambling. John tossed the TV remote and looked at his watch. Perhaps if he waited and went back down at midnight? He crushed the butt in the already full ashtray and went to take a shower. That would kill enough time and clear his head.

The warm water massaged his tired body. He wanted to wash away all his regrets and start over; this was the last chance at salvation. If he hit it big, perhaps then he could redeem himself in the eyes of his lost family. John told himself he did it for them, for a chance at a better life than his middle class income could afford. He told himself the same lie for the last fifteen years.

He got out of the shower and wiped the steam off the mirror. Jumping back, he slipped on the wet floor and crashed to the ground. His hands flew to touch his face, not the one he just saw in the mirror.

"I must be tired." John rubbed his jaw feeling the stubble run along his palm like sandpaper and rubbed his eyes. He pushed himself up and took a deep breath. The glass had fogged over again, and he cleared it with a trembling hand. Exhaling now he said, "Thank God." John shook his head and wondered why he imagined himself burned; his face charred and black with bits of flesh falling off in gruesome lumps.

After quickly dressing, he grabbed the pillow. He stood for only a moment with the money in his hand before he shoved it into his wallet and left the room again. This time he would not be back in his room until morning. It took six hours to win a decent amount, but less than thirty minutes to give it all back. He had won, but not enough. It had never been enough. He wanted to hit it big, just this once, and promised never to gamble again.

John trudged over to the chair and lifted the seat cushion. The last of his money remained safely folded. He snatched it and turned for the door, stopping after only three steps. His fist clenched around the bills. John didn't feel his finger nails digging into his flesh, only the warm money pressed inside his palm.

He needed strength and said, "Put the goddamn money back. You have two more days."

His grip loosened and he took the three long steps back to return the money. He never made it to the bed, but collapsed into the chair. Silent tears filled his restless sleep.

It was some time later that he awoke, and his eyes squinted as he looked around the sun filled room. Recollection seeped into his consciousness, and he quickly reached under the cushion to feel for the money. Breathing a sigh of relief, he stretched his sore muscles. "Today's the day; I know it."

He shaved and took a fast shower. The duffel bag still sat on top of the pristine bed, and he put his leisure suit, not caring that it needed to be pressed. Grabbing the last of his cash, he told himself that this will be his lucky day.

John's stomach grumbled as he sat in the coffee shop aimlessly rolling the coin across his knuckles. His thoughts drifted to his and Gloria's last argument over a year ago now; he hocked his daughter's flute for some fast cash to bet on a sure thing. He could still hear his wife's sobbing words,

Tales from the Silver State IV

"I've had enough! First our house, then Laura's college fund. Now she has to quit band."

He couldn't quite make eye contact and stammered out, "I promise it won't happen again."

"I'm tired of your promises." She wiped her eyes, smearing black mascara across her face.

"Please, I'll get everything back for you and Laura. I'll do anything."

She took a slow breath and asked, "Will you quit gambling?"

John answered with silence.

Her face reddened concealing her freckles. "You love to gamble more than you love us. Get out!"

If he could just hit it big he would buy his daughter an entire orchestra. Hell, he would pay for anywhere she wants to go to school and even get his ex-wife a new house to try and make-up for everything he'd lost.

The waitress placed the steak and eggs in front of him and asked, "anything else you need?"

John nodded at her, "No, I'm fine." And he told himself he would be after today.

Tales from the Silver State IV

He left a five-dollar bill on the table and went to pay for his $1.99 meal. In the casino, he got that same feeling that kids have on the night before Christmas. All the lights blinking on the machines were John's Christmas tree.

This was his last chance. He got his favorite spot, third base, and began. At first playing it smart, but as the pile of chips grew in front of him, so did his excitement. It didn't take long before his hunches cost him all his winnings and what he started with for the day.

He sat for a moment staring at his last hand of a jack, three and king. As the dealer cleared the cards he said, "Better luck next time, sir."

John reached into his pocket, but didn't have any bills left. He needed a drink and sulked over to some slot machines on the far end of the casino and sat down. It wasn't long before a cocktail waitress came over. "What'll you have, Sugar?"

"Gin and tonic." John tried to smile and added, "make it a double please."

"Sure, Honey." She said kindly and didn't add the good luck, knowing he was tapped out.

John massaged his lucky coin between his fingers and remembered the day he got it; the first time he felt the thrill of gambling. His older brother bet him on a Yankee's game. Now Tom was dead, and John was having thoughts about joining him. He closed his eyes and made a silent prayer, *I'll give anything to win big, just once.*

John stared at the quarter lost in a world of desperate hope and misery when a velvety voice broke his train of thought. "Why don't you play it?" A beautiful woman sat only inches from him.

His mouth opened to say something, but he could only gaze into her deep black eyes. Her perfect full lips smiled at him as she waited for a reply. "Um. I never play this. It's my lucky coin."

She laughed, "If that's the case, you should play it, right?" She reached over and touched his arm. A rush of adrenaline filled his body. "I'll be your good luck charm."

In trance-like motion he put the quarter into the machine and pulled the handle. It spun round and round landing on three 7's. The coins were a magnificent orchestra as they tumbled down, sounding better than the Boston Philharmonic to him.

"See, I told you." Her slender eyebrow rose. "Your prayers have been answered."

Tales from the Silver State IV

John was too lost in the rush of winning to comprehend the implication of her remark. "Thank you!" He grabbed a bucket and started filling it with quarters. "Here, fill one for yourself."

"No, the money is all for you, John. And this is just the beginning."

That was odd; he didn't remember telling her his name. "What's your name?" he asked.

"Oh, I go by many names. Why don't you call me Lucy?" She brushed a strand of bright red hair away from her ivory face.

The waitress came as the coins finished their song. "Looks like your luck changed, Honey."

"Yes, yes it did." John filled her tray with quarters and downed the drink. With some liquid courage he turned to Lucy and asked, "I'm going to cash these in for chips, would you like to join me?"

"But of course. Why else am I here, John?"

She draped her arm through his. As they walked to the cashier, every man's gaze followed them, looking at her. John's head was high and his spirits higher. He was right; this was his lucky day.

Tales from the Silver State IV

He was hot, winning at every table. All the while Lucy stood quietly by his side. When it was almost midnight, he had won more than he ever imagined possible.

"It's time for me to go now."

He knew when she left so would his winning streak. "Will I see you again?"

She smirked, "But of course, John. That was the deal."

As he watched her walk away, for a split second she looked inhuman. His mouth went dry and sweat formed on the back of his neck. He ran his fingers through his hair and told himself he was tired and had too much booze.

John stumbled into his room and pushed the duffel bag off the bed. He fell across it, not bothering to even take off his shoes. He wouldn't awake until early morning.

In a state between dream and reality, he first heard the screams. His heavy eyelids struggled to open. When they did, he saw his room filled with smoke, swirling in long tendrils from the air vent.

A familiar voice purred in the mist, "Time to pay up, John."

"What the Hell?"

Tales from the Silver State IV

Her eerie laughter filled the room. "I see you do understand."

He covered his mouth and ran for the door. The hallway was void of light and filled with smoke and bodies lying on the ground. John slammed the door shut and rushed to the window. The cry of sirens wailed outside. His muscles strained against the glass, but it didn't budge.

"What are you doing, John?" She chuckled, "There is no way out. You are mine now."

He coughed out, "What are you talking about?"

"We made a deal, John."

He grabbed the chair and thrust it against the window. It broke and he pushed his head through the jagged glass. Black smoke filled the sky, and curtains flapped in the cool breeze like dying birds.

Her hot breath brushed against the back of his neck, "Care to jump?"

"Go to Hell, Lady."

The feminine laughter morphed into a deep baritone that shook the room. "With you at my side."

John looked up into the terror filled sky and prayed. *Please, God. Let me make this right first. Please.*

Tales from the Silver State IV

He couldn't control his coughing and the room started to spin. John crashed to the floor. A brilliant ray of light broke through the darkness and cascaded into the room. He closed his eyes.

When he opened them again he was in a hospital hallway filled with gurneys. He could barely breath, even with the oxygen mask on him, and lifted his hand to get someone's attention.

A man turned from another fire victim and walked over to John. He leaned in close and asked, "What can I do for you, my son?"

John looked into his face, lined like a well-worn map, and whispered, "I need to make it right."

The priest knew too well there wasn't much time left. He took out a pad and pencil and wrote down John's final words giving his ex-wife and daughter all his winnings.

Redemption had come at the highest price.

THE PROMISE OF THE WHITE BUFFALO
by Noëlle de Beaufort

The White Buffalo Calf
The Spirit Ethers

Hear me. Find me. Save me.

*****

Red Sunset
Great Basin High-Desert Plain, Nevada
Early Spring 1826

I hear whispers, but see nothing but a foggy mist of waves. Sitting cross-legged within a ritual circle of rocks, an auburn-haired Paiute woman chanted. *The image is shimmering, clearing.* Before an ebbing orange-flamed fire, under the sparkling radiance of stars white as pearls in the midnight sky, she swayed in a circular motion as visions washed over her consciousness. She opened her eyes. *I hear you. I will find you. I will save you.* The Paiute mystic, shaman of the Snow Tribe, raised her hands to the Great Spirit, spoke the sacred words, and lowered her head toward her heart.

*****

French Buffalo

Tales from the Silver State IV

Chief French Buffalo, called *Bagootsoo Fran-say* by his Paiute tribe, sat at a respectful distance from his mother, Red Sunset, named *Taba U-we-ka Atsa* in her native language, while she communed with the spirit world. His birth father, a French fur trapper and adventurer known as *Shan-loo-ee,* the phonic translation of Jean-Louis, leaned back on one elbow.

A year earlier, Jean-Louis had returned to the Snow Tribe, after an absence of more than forty years, to learn that he had a son. They had forged a bond immediately as men of action.

The young chief felt apprehensive about his tribe's future in a changing world. Protected from raids of other tribes due to their snow-peaked mountain refuge with natural barriers to conquest, French Buffalo had come to understand more of the conflicts of men by hearing his father's stories of life beyond their high-mountain camp. Jean-Louis contended that the Snow Tribe's path to survival lay not in war, but in trade and treaties with the white man. A clear-thinking man, the chief was mindful of *Shan-loo-ee's* warning: "White men lie. Money motivates them above all else. Learn their language, understand their ways and beat them at their own game. If not, their sheer numbers will bury you and your culture for all time."

Already the old ways were threatened by the incursion of occasional bands of white men. When the Paiute hunted buffalo, as recently as French Buffalo's childhood, herds filled the high-desert plains. All parts of the buffalo were harvested. Hides were worked for *tipis* and clothing, the carcass butchered for food, the horns and bones carved and shaped for implements or ornaments. Lately, braves had reported seeing dead buffalo carcasses putrefying, unbutchered. He saw that white men hunted for sport, not for survival. Their wagons moved over the plains as canoes through a river.

After a trance, Red Sunset never spoke until she had slept. After she entered the *tipi,* French Buffalo lay for a while under the stars, thoughts rolling through his mind. *Should his children follow the ways of the ancestors or the ways of the white man? Could they live in both worlds? Could he?*

*****

Jean-Louis

An unnatural stillness awoke Jean-Louis near dawn. *The best time for animals to hunt.* Although sheltered in a *tipi,* he avoided any abrupt move. He slowly opened one eye. Sour sweat dripped from his forehead and neck. He glanced at Red Sunset sleeping by his side, the lover who had haunted his dreams for more than forty years. Their son was awake; their eyes met. Jean-Louis touched Red Sunset on the lips, a signal to remain still.

None stirred.

The sound of paws padding over the still-frosted ground as the cougar circled their *tipi* continued for a few minutes, then receded. *She could be lying in wait.* Jean-Louis knew that horses feared sudden movements, not silent predators like cougars who blended into their surroundings. She would pounce before the horses could pull away from their tethers.

Both Jean-Louis and French Buffalo reached for their bows and quivers, sliding silently over the buffalo hide covering the ground until they reached the outer edge of the *tipi*, lifting the hide enclosing their refuge a mere inch or two. *Nothing*. Slowly, deliberately, they moved around the inner perimeter until they had performed a complete reconnaissance of the external threat to determine her location. They crept out of the *tipi*, shouting Paiute war whoops to spook the cougar. She sped away in a flash of tan, sprays of snow sparking from her paws.

In a delayed reaction, the horses strained at their ties. Jean-Louis and French Buffalo rubbed the long necks of their mounts, speaking in soft, soothing voices to calm them.

As the morning's breaking light obscured the canopy of stars above, Jean-Louis rested his hand on his son's shoulder. "I am glad we had this quiet time before journeying over the new trade route. It will be faster and more lucrative for our tribe to trade our furs in San Francisco instead of Ft. Vancouver. We shall discover this city on the Pacific together."

Red Sunset emerged from the *tipi*. "Come, let us eat and talk." French Buffalo fed the horses, while Jean-Louis revived the campfire and Red Sunset brought out the morning's provisions.

Tales from the Silver State IV

The sun illuminated white streaks in the once-dark auburn hair of Red Sunset. She sipped water infused with a tincture of berries she had created to achieve the ideal mixture of sweetness and tartness. "The Great Spirit has shown me a white buffalo calf."

Jean-Louis squinted into the sun and then turned his head toward Red Sunset, tilting his head, puzzled.

French Buffalo raised his hands to the sky. "It is a message from the Great Spirit. A white buffalo calf is the promise of protection and good fortune. It is a rare gift to glimpse one."

The shaman nodded. "The white buffalo calf spoke to me. He needs our help. We must find him. He is in some kind of danger."

"Where will we find this calf? His mother will be protective. I have seen more than one hunter gored by these ill-tempered, fast-running animals." Jean-Louis swallowed the remaining contents of his cup. "And what will we do with this white buffalo calf after we find him?"

Red Sunset smiled at her lover. "The portents will guide us."

"You mean now? On our way back to the mountain, we will find this white buffalo calf?" Although Jean-Louis had never known Red Sunset to err, they had not seen a gang of buffalo for days. "Buffalo roam farther to the east, not on our trail home."

Tales from the Silver State IV

The mystical shaman stood. "We will find him."

French Buffalo rose to his feet. "Let us break camp and be on our way."

Jean-Louis shrugged in surrender.

*****

Red Sunset

The first day of travel passed without incident. The second day, as they approached the low forests at the base of Snow Mountain, howls punctuated with grunts diverted their attention from the trail.

Pulling up on his horse's reins, French Buffalo pointed toward an outcropping of rocks near a meandering stream. He and Jean-Louis rode ahead, motioning to Red Sunset to wait. She felt the call of the white buffalo calf, and moved toward the rocks despite their admonition to hold her position.

When Red Sunset reached a point where she could observe and remain safe, she saw Jean-Louis and their son driving a pack of gray wolves away from a lone buffalo, who lay on her side, writhing in mid-calving. Wounds on her head and chest appeared grave, though two dead wolves, one gored through the skull and the other through its groin, sprawled nearby. After the remaining wolves raced away, Jean-Louis jumped off his horse and approached the suffering mother.

"Stop!" French Buffalo shouted at his father from horseback. "She may rise and attack!"

Tales from the Silver State IV

"The calf is coming out legs first. We will have to cut him out of her or he will die. She is as good as dead."

Red Sunset chanted, and the calving buffalo calmed.

"We must birth the calf, and get him to milk immediately, before she dies. He must nurse directly after birth or he will not live." French Buffalo knew the ways of the buffalo herds from years of hunting. "Even so, I have only seen one survive being born of a near-dead mother." The chief dismounted and walked toward the dying buffalo.

Jean-Louis knelt next to the mother, and looked directly into her eyes.

She appeared to see him, stilled her shaking and lowered her head to rest on the ground. He whispered, "Forgive me. Your calf must live." In one swift move, he slipped a long-knife from his boot and sliced open the mother's womb, pulling out a blood-soaked white calf. It lay still until Jean-Louis slapped its chest. After emitting a brief grunt, the calf breathed. Its eyes remained shut.

French Buffalo helped Jean-Louis position the calf to nurse. As the calf suckled, the mother's visible eye closed.

"The milk will flow as long as the calf feeds. Then we should try to fill a water pouch with more until we can get back to camp and supplement his nourishment with the milk of our mountain goats." Red Sunset emptied a water pouch and gathered some grasses by the stream where the tribe harvested wild rice in autumn.

Tales from the Silver State IV

After the calf had fed and rolled off his mother, the newborn struggled to stand while Red Sunset filled the pouch with milk. The calf finally stood, walked with an uneven gait and touched his milk-stained nose to his mother's brow. After a few moments, he waddled over to Red Sunset and held his head next to her heart. She looked into his expectant eyes. She heard a response in her mind.

I called to you. I knew you would save me. I bring wisdom, protection and good fortune.

*****

French Buffalo
Camp of the Snow Tribe

Elders filed into the *wicki-up* of Chief French Buffalo where he, Jean-Louis and Red Sunset greeted them. They sat in a circle, intoning prayers and passing a pipe of crushed herbs, known as the Pipe of Mystic Flight. Its essence transported smokers to a higher plane where their ancestors imparted knowledge. As one, the group swayed and chanted. When French Buffalo clapped his hands, they stopped. "The wisdom of our ancestors and the white buffalo calf will guide us toward our future. The ways of the ancestors are the true ways of the heart. Change comes to all things under the sun, moon and stars. We must learn from the white man, adapt, and protect our way of life."

A white-braided sun-wizened elder disagreed. "Our camp is high, already protected by its sheer cliffs. Only we know the paths. The white man will never attack our camp."

Tales from the Silver State IV

Another nodded. "If we continue to bring the white man furs, they will stay away. They are lazy."

Jean-Louis inhaled the smoke, passed the pipe and spoke. "It is true the Snow Tribe is protected by geography. The fur trade works in our favor now. We can expand it and thrive. For now. But the white man's wagon trains will keep coming. Do not mistake practicality for laziness. Most men avoid war if they can get what they want in another way. Their drive west, to the Pacific Ocean, will continue. Our best hope is to trade in peace with the white man. Not all white men we encounter will be peaceful; the goodwill we establish now must be strong enough to gain protection of the wise white men against the unwise."

A former rival of French Buffalo spoke. "I had nothing but disdain for *Shan-loo-ee* when he came back to our tribe. But now I think he speaks truth. The white buffalo calf promises protection, but we must seize that promise like a rope thrown to a fallen brave below the cliff's edge – it is the only way forward."

French Buffalo looked directly at each elder. "I believe we must learn their ways or surely we will be extinguished like the embers of a dying fire."

The elders murmured among themselves, voted in agreement with the chief, stood and left. The oldest one, the white-braided elder, stopped and put his hand on French Buffalo's shoulder. "A wise chief listens. We will follow you."

Tales from the Silver State IV

French Buffalo's wife, Mountain Moon, whose Paiute name was *Muha To-ya-be*, did not attend the tribal council. The only woman ever permitted to attend was Red Sunset, due to her unique status as shaman of the tribe.

After the council, Mountain Moon entered their *wicki-up* and sat on the ground. "Our children sit with the white buffalo calf while he sleeps." *Tso-a-pu Oha*, their daughter, was called Yellow Butterfly in white man's language, and their son, *Bagootsoo Poohe* was known as Blue Buffalo. He had the same blue eyes as his grandfather, *Shan-loo-ee*.

"Yellow Butterfly says the white buffalo calf comes to her in visions. His name is Snow Star *Ne-ba-be Ta-se-no*." Mountain Moon sighed. "Blue Buffalo closes his eyes tightly and tries to meld his mind with that of the white buffalo calf, but does not succeed in summoning visions. He stomps off in anger."

French Buffalo twirled a stick around the fire's edge. "Our daughter has visions like her grandmother, the gift of long-sight. Our son has the gift of healing, like his uncle Red Buffalo, *Bagootsoo Atsa*. He knows instinctively the particular herb to harvest and mix with tinctures to cure each affliction. Their gifts are of equal measure. I will speak to him." He paused for a moment. "I believe we should consider sending the children to study the white man's ways."

Red Sunset looked at Jean-Louis. They remained silent until Mountain Moon had spoken.

Tales from the Silver State IV

Mountain Moon whispered, "No!"

Jean-Louis shifted his position and leaned forward. "You have not spoken of this before."

French Buffalo tilted his head. "I have listened to your stories of Canada, of London, of New York and your way west. Adventurous members of our tribe have ventured to Canada, to Ft. Vancouver, to the Great Basin Desert and to nearby trading posts. These are wide boundaries, but narrow as well. I have never seen a city as you have described. Our children," he looked at Mountain Moon, "may need to know more in order to survive. Our way of life may not last. I think the white buffalo calf is here to provide us protection, as well as a path to the future. Could not the white buffalo calf be a sign to look beyond our tribe? Think on it, and we will talk when I return from San Francisco."

A single tear stained Mountain Moon's cheek.

*****

Jean-Louis
The trail to San Francisco

The packhorses, laden with furs of rabbit, beaver, raccoon, fox and mink, were led over steep trails curving around the Sierra Nevada. At night, the trail iced up, but melted before they broke camp. The two-hundred-mile trip over the mountains to the coast was about a third of the distance they had previously traveled to trade in Ft. Vancouver. It could be covered in a little more than a week, rather than three, promising to be a faster and more lucrative trade route for the tribe.

Jean-Louis and French Buffalo rode at the head of the packhorses and two braves rode at the end of the rope-linked train. About the time that Jean-Louis gauged they were two days away from San Francisco, they heard a voice crying out for help.

French Buffalo signaled to the braves behind to stop and guard the packhorses. He and Jean-Louis dismounted to investigate, one hand on their knives. Their cargo was valuable. An ambush might await them.

They followed the weak voices, and found three bodies by a campfire, one moved, moaning in pain. Jean-Louis knelt by the wounded man, whose rough brown robe identified him as a friar. "What happened?"

"Bears. We thought the fire would repel them." He coughed. Blood spurted from his mouth.

"Not this time of year. " Jean-Louis cradled the man's head." Bears are awakening from hibernation. Their drive for food is at its maximum. Your provisions attracted them and sealed your fate."

"Fate? No, sir, we are missionaries of the Catholic church. Fate is for non-believers. Somewhere Jesus has a purpose for us in our deaths."

Jean-Louis shook his head in frustration. "Jesus had nothing to do with it. You camped in the woods without knowing enough about wildlife. This is their territory, not man's."

The priest fought to speak, but could not utter a word.

"Breathe a bit."

The man's breaths came slowly, and his eyes cleared from their glassy stare.

Knowing the friar had but minutes to live, Jean-Louis pressed on. "Who are you? Who can we tell of your deaths?"

"The mission in San Francisco. I am Friar José." The coughs came more frequently, but he lifted his head, unwilling to succumb. "My sons," he looked at both the trapper and the Paiute, "let me bless you…redeem you from your sins before I die."

The French trapper's expression hardened. "I seek no redemption from any priest. My sins are my own and shall remain so."

Reaching toward French Buffalo, the priest's bloody hand touched him. "But you, my son, a heathen, you must be saved or you will burn in hell. This man," he glanced toward Jean-Louis, "has chosen to forsake God. But you can still save your soul."

French Buffalo shook his head and placed his hand on the man's red-stained fingers in a gentle grip. "My soul rests in the Great Spirit. We are all one under the Big Sky. The Great Spirit will take your soul and you will be as a star in the heavens forever."

"Blasphemy!" The priest sputtered blood. "Heathen!"

Tales from the Silver State IV

Jean-Louis put his finger over the man's lips. "Go in peace, not in anger. See to your own soul. We will see to ours, Friar José. Redeem yourself."

The dying man blinked and Jean-Louis thought understanding sparked in the priest's eyes the moment before the death stare transfixed him.

French Buffalo pulled a shovel from a packhorse to dig three shallow graves. Jean-Louis wielded an axe to chop down a small tree and used long grasses as ties to form three crosses. Two were blank. On the last, he carved "Fr. José."

The chief watched and said. "Why are you doing this?"

"The cross is a symbol of their religion. The mission will dispatch a party to recover the bodies for reburial in consecrated ground. They do not burn dead flesh as you do, gathering up bones after the body has been consumed by fire."

French Buffalo looked at his father. "I would learn the white man's letters."

Jean-Louis nodded. "I will teach you."

"And my children. All the tribe's children will learn the white man's letters."

"Your children are yours to raise. But the elders may resist the entire tribe learning to read."

"I can be persuasive. Do you doubt me?"

Jean-Louis laughed and shook his head in resignation. "Not from what I've seen so far."

Tales from the Silver State IV

Resuming their ride, French Buffalo was silent for an hour, then asked, "What is this 'hell' that the friar said I would burn in?"

Jean-Louis shook his head. "Men look for ways to control other men. It has been so since the dawn of time. Hell is a myth of eternal fire and damnation, punishment for blasphemy. Blasphemy is a word that means not believing what another man believes. The notion of hell strikes fear in those with no connection to the Great Spirit. In truth, Friar José met hell when he met the bear."

Looking directly at French Buffalo, he continued, "There is no burning lake of hellfire. The mind of man constructs its own hell, its own prisons to punish itself."

French Buffalo looked off into the distance. "I have much to learn. For years, I wondered who you were, where you were, and why you did not stay. I know you followed your own path, and now that it has led you back to us, it warms my heart. But truly, I think the Great Spirit sent you to us, as he sent the white buffalo calf. There is a purpose to it. We need your guidance. I need your guidance."

Jean-Louis looked at his son. "I never knew you existed. Your mother and the man who raised you guided you well. You are a fine man. I always planned to return, so perhaps the time was right. For the new world you face, I have knowledge that might help. We shall face it together."

*****

White Buffalo Calf

Tales from the Silver State IV

Camp of the Snow Tribe

Yellow Butterfly and Blue Buffalo sat across from the white buffalo calf as he slept.

Blue Buffalo jumped to his feet and stared at his sister. "What did you say?"

Yellow Butterfly looked confused. "Nothing."

"You told me to find the flower with purple nettles and pink centers."

"I did not!"

"Well, then," he looked around, "who is talking to me?"

"No one else is here." She shrugged, stared at the white buffalo calf then looked at Blue Buffalo with wide eyes. "It was Snow Star! He spoke in your head! I can *see* things! You can *hear* things!"

Blue Buffalo frowned and tilted his head.

"Don't be confused." The voice in his head was clear. "I show her visions, I send you words. Go find the flower, pull it up by the root and bring it back here."

The boy jumped to his feet and ran to find the flowering herb.

Yellow Butterfly followed him, calling out, "Where are you going?"

"He told me to find the flower, the one with purple nettles and pink centers. They are up by the cave where Grandfather *Shan-loo-ee* hid when he first came to our tribe. Come on!"

Tales from the Silver State IV

The children flew over the rocky terrain, sure-footed as mules.

Yellow Butterfly stopped and pointed. "It's over there. I saw a flash of purple and pink by that tree."

Following her lead, Blue Buffalo walked in back of the tree and found the plants. He looked at her. "You couldn't have seen this flower; it was hidden by the tree."

"Snow Star showed it to me."

The boy pulled out one flower by its roots and both children went back to see their wild friend, who was still sleeping.

"He's asleep." Blue Buffalo's voice conveyed his disappointment.

"I know you found the flower." The words were clear in Blue Buffalo's head. "Take it to Red Sunset and tell her to mash the nettles and mix in the amount that covers one fingertip into a full pouch of goat's milk. That will give me nourishment."

When they arrived at Red Sunset's *wicki-up*, she hugged her grandchildren and took the flower. "I've been waiting for you to bring me what Snow Star needs."

*****

French Buffalo
Near the end of the trail to San Francisco

Breaking camp along the trail, Jean-Louis and French Buffalo prepared the packhorses laden with furs for the last day of their trading mission trek to San Francisco.

Tales from the Silver State IV

French Buffalo thought of the future as they rode toward their destination. His responsibilities were clear in his mind. *The tribe must survive.*

The horse train advanced around a hill to reveal an unobstructed vista to the Pacific Ocean.

French Buffalo gasped in awe.

"A marvelous sight, is it not?" Jean-Louis glanced at French Buffalo and smiled, before turning his eyes back to what lay ahead.

Transfixed, French Buffalo's eyes scanned the scene below. Permanent dwellings of stone spread out in all directions. People, as small from this vantage point as the industrious ants they resembled, swarmed about. Tall ships in the harbor sported sails of many colors.

Jean-Louis laughed and reached out to playfully hit his son on the shoulder. "A new world, eh?"

Tales from the Silver State IV

THE VIRGAE
by Jay Hill

The law firm was on the top floor of a mid-rise office tower in Summerlin and, in the early evening, it was empty except for a late-staying receptionist, the lawyer and Hector Garcia. The lawyer looked like all lawyers, and Hector Garcia was squat with his face and hands dark from the sun and his black curls thin and salted with gray.

The lawyer led Hector down a hall decorated with original art. The carpet was thick and plush with the pile aligned from vacuuming. Hector wore black leather work shoes, wrinkled, free of dirt and mud, but dusty from leaves and cut grass; the heels needed repair, but the soles were thick with a heavy tread that would outlast the uppers. Hector took short, quick steps, nimble-walking on the outside edges of his shoes to avoid marking the carpet.

The lawyer's office was on the east side of the building. Hector sat in a chair facing south and the lawyer. The lawyer sat behind his desk facing north and Hector. Diplomas, licenses, and awards covered the wall behind the lawyer. The lawyer's desk was neat and clean with a desk pad, a picture frame, and a clock. The frame and the clock faced the lawyer, and Hector guessed that the frame held a photo of the lawyer's family. Hector did not have a wall of certificates or a desk or an office.

To Hector's left was an east facing window wall; the late day sun lit The Strip; beyond it, the Mud Mountains were bare and dull brown with the bright, dry air magnifying the Valley. Artwork, chosen to confirm the lawyer's sophistication, decorated the remaining walls.

Hector gave his documents to the lawyer. The lawyer looked at them, shuffled them several times, and leaned forward; his disciplined eyes projected care and concern and concealed his predatory focus.

"You have a serious problem, Mr. Garcia," the lawyer said.

"I didn't do anything wrong," Hector said.

"Mr. Garcia, the DMV standard form DUI report says your BAC was 0.10."

"I was sitting there, stopped, my driving was perfect."

"That doesn't matter. The legislature revised the DUI statute, NRS 484C.110, and eliminated subjective defenses, mens rea, intent, actual behavior, or proof of driving impairment. It's a criminal act for any person who has a concentration of alcohol of 0.08 or more in his or her blood or breath to drive or be in actual physical control of a vehicle on a highway or on premises to which the public has access. I'll be glad to read you the statute."

"It's the drunk's fault. He was on the wrong side of the median strip."

Tales from the Silver State IV

"I searched the Clerk of Courts' records on the internet and found the Nevada Uniform Traffic Tag for the other driver. His BAC was 0.09 and Metro cited him for DUI, failure to control, and left of center. Unfortunately, none of that exonerates you."

"I pulled up to the intersection, stopped and was waiting for my turn."

"And drunk hits you head on - That's bad luck."

"He was on the wrong side of the median."

"I noticed that you refused the psycho-motor tests."

"I would have done okay."

"The report states that you said that they weren't required and were subjective."

"That's right."

"Where did you learn that?"

"I heard it."

"In a bar?"

"From an attorney."

"You have a DUI that isn't showing up?"

"Many years ago."

"It should come up. How many years?"

"Another lifetime."

"Another state?"

"California and another name and social. I got deported under it."

"What's your real name?"

Tales from the Silver State IV

"This, now; I got straight this time; came in under a family reunion exemption."

"And you recalled that psycho-motors aren't required?"

"The lawyer said they weren't fair; that the cops say you failed when you didn't."

"What lawyer?"

"He was on TV with a funny mustache."

"Jack Kremer?"

"That's it. You know him?"

"I grew up in California. It was excellent advice then, but not now."

"He said they had to prove you couldn't drive."

"They had to prove impairment, but now it's about the number you blow."

"That sucks."

"How well you drove doesn't matter."

"The car wasn't moving."

"The motor was running, and you were behind the wheel. The statute says 'drive or be in actual physical control of a vehicle on a highway or on premises to which the public has access.'"

"It's not fair."

"We're in court two weeks from Thursday. If you can't pay now, have my fee in cash."

"Can you get me off?"

"We'll pull the full breath report and check the device calibration log."

"If they're not okay?"

"We'll file a demand for a jury trial and get a pre-trial conference."

"Otherwise?"

"We'll enter a plea, and I'll get you the best possible result."

"A guilty plea?"

"No contest; it's like a guilty plea, but it protects you if the other driver sues."

"So, I'm screwed? My driving doesn't matter?"

"It's like a parking ticket. Lawyers call it the elimination of mens rea, but the legislature eliminated the need for any proof of actual impairment."

"It's not fair. I didn't do anything wrong. I have to drive my truck."

"I'll get you work privileges."

Hector got up. He stopped and stared at the print by the door.

"Is he dying?" he asked.

"It's called The Wounded Man," the lawyer said.

"He doesn't look too good," Hector said.

"It's a self-portrait."

"He painted himself stabbed?"

"It was the artist with his lover, but she left with their children, and he painted over her."

"That would hurt."

Tales from the Silver State IV

"The wound is metaphorical; the painting is a famous pentimento or in French repentir."

The lawyer liked to say repentir more than mens rea.

"To lose your children would be terrible."

"It's substantial emotional pain and distress and psychological trauma."

"Did he get them back?"

"I have no idea," said the lawyer, "No one has ever asked me that."

The lawyer walked Hector to the door and reminded him of payment. The two men shook hands and agreed to meet outside the courtroom.

Hector took the elevator to the first floor and, confronted with four identical exits, chose the wrong exit and discovered that he could not re-enter the building. Hector walked around the building without complaint because Hector always "walked around the building." Security stopped Hector, but let him go after warning him that it was too late to be landscaping.

The lawyer returned to his office and sat in his chair; his hands trembled, he was sick to his stomach and wanted to leave, but suppressed the urge. The lawyer fantasized that Hector had activated a vindictive entity within the lawyer; that it was his own malevolence, an auto-immune disease of his soul, that threatened to become him, and the lawyer propped up his fragile self with the lie, which he knew was a lie - that his symptoms came from excess coffee.

Tales from the Silver State IV

The lawyer steepled his elbows and hands, rested his chin on his fingers, and sucked in air. His body quivered; his vision narrowed. The lawyer diagnosed his panic as manageable and his agitation and end-of-the-world-need-to-crawl-out-of-my-skin anxiety as transient symptoms.

The lawyer got a bottle of lorazepam from his briefcase, shook several tablets onto his desk blotter and placed two on his tongue. He fished a discarded water bottle from his trash can and gulped down the tablets.

The lawyer leaned back with his clothes damp and his back tight. He replayed his conference with Hector but omitted the pentimento discussion because it was not relevant.

The lawyer called his ex-wife on her cell and said, "I may be fifteen minutes late."

She said, "Remember what the mediator said - the world doesn't revolve around you."

"I had an attack."

"Deal with it," she said, "We have two children who don't care about your attacks."

Hector and the lawyer stood before the Judge, and the Judge asked for Hector's plea. The lawyer said, "No Contest, Your Honor."

The Judge read a litany of warnings and ended by asking, "You understand that by pleading No Contest you admit the facts stated in the Complaint, and if those facts constitute the elements of an offense, I will find you guilty?"

Tales from the Silver State IV

Hector said, "I didn't do anything wrong. My driving was perfect."

The Judge said, "Mr. Garcia, I cannot accept a No Contest plea if you deny guilt and assert your innocence."

The lawyer said, "He will plead, Your Honor. He's having a difficult time."

The Judge said, "Exercise better client control counselor. Sort this out and get back on the docket when you're ready."

In the hallway, the lawyer said, "Pleading is your best option. Enter the plea, agree to the facts and accept the result."

Hector's wife said, "Hector, do what he says. We'll get through this together."

Hector looked at the floor and stood silent. He looked at his wife; she nodded her head "yes."

Hector looked at the lawyer and said, "Okay, I'll do it."

The lawyer said, "No changeups. Let's do this. Any more time and my fee increases."

Hector looked at his wife; she saw Hector's eyes dull and tired and that she and Hector had grown apart, and she felt sad, and Hector saw what his wife saw.

The lawyer and Hector stood before the Judge a second time.

The Judge asked, "Counselor, do you have your package ready?"

Hector said, "I am a person."

Tales from the Silver State IV

The lawyer said, "I do, Your Honor, and we waive the standard cautions."

"I can't do that," the Judge said, and he again recited the litany of warnings and ended with, "You understand that by pleading No Contest you admit the facts stated in the Complaint, and if those facts constitute the elements of an offense, I will find you guilty?"

Hector said, "I have done no wrong. I work hard, and I care for my family."

The Judge said, "Counselor, you have a problem."

Hector looked up, stared at the Judge. Hector's face contorted, went limp and, with his final exhale, Hector made a sound that the Judge would come to know was a death rattle.

Hector experienced a massive cerebral hemorrhage resulting in Hector's instant unconsciousness and death. Hector's corpse arced forward into the space between the court reporter's stenotype machine and the witness box. Gravity pulled Hector's face into the short pile courtroom carpet and the concrete beneath it. Hector's nose snapped with a sharp crack and his right zygomatic bone shattered, but it was of no consequence to Hector as he had ceased to exist.

The coroner said that Hector's aneurysm doomed him regardless of circumstance; if he were trimming an oleander or buying mulch or eating lunch, the result would be the same; but Hector wasn't doing any of those things. Hector stood before the Judge, and the Judge couldn't forget Hector's words or the look on Hector's face or Hector's last exhale or Hector falling toward him or the pop of Hector's nose snapping.

Hector's death was courthouse gossip for three days and forgotten.

Hector's survivors expressed appropriate grief and anguish, and his widow cared for his grave until her body lay beside Hector's.

The lawyer practiced law and had panic attacks with his children and ex-wife uncaring. His colleagues celebrated and honored him, and he was discontent and never satisfied.

The Judge dismissed Hector's case, and his clerk marked "DDD" on the front of the case file with a wide black marker; it was unknown whether "DDD" stood for "Dismissed Due to Death" or "Dismissed due to Death of Defendant" or "Dismissed Defendant Dead" and it made no difference to Hector or anyone.

The Judge's application of the law in Hector's case was exemplary, but confronted with Hector-like litigants; the Judge experienced faint terror and heartburn. Acid blockers prevented this annoyance and, after the Judge's bypass surgery, it disappeared.

During the first year of the Judge's final term in office, Hector Garcia began to appear to the Judge. The Judge would see a translucent Hector Garcia standing before him and mouthing, "I am a person . . . I am a person . . . ," until

Tales from the Silver State IV

Hector fell forward; and Hector should have fallen into the Judge, but like rain falling through desert air, Hector evaporated and touched nothing and no one.

Tales from the Silver State IV

THE MAN WHO THREW A SHOVEL AT GOD
by John Hill

Dr. Jeffrey Fields, 38, golfing with friends on that Saturday in April, 1968, was a happy man, with peace of mind, and why not, with a family he treasured, a fulfilling, successful medical practice, a new big two-story Tudor-style home on several wooded acres in a prosperous suburb of Kansas City, when got the phone call that murdered his life.

He'd been rushed to the clubhouse for the phone call, by an older black caddy, furiously driving up in a golf cart, bouncing up over the 11th hole, saying there was an emergency phone call for the doctor. Apologizing to his golf buddies, Dr. Jeffrey Fields had sighed, got in the cart, and was rushed back to the main office of the clubhouse, wondering which patient had an emergency. He did care about each of them. It was why he became a doctor, to help. He was a good man. And he knew he was blessed.

At the clubhouse, he was directed to the club office and picked up the phone.

"Dr. Jeffrey Fields."

"Dr. Fields, this is Det. Mack Hail, Overland Park homicide. We need you to come right to Overland Park Memorial Hospital please. It is located off —"

Tales from the Silver State IV

"I know where it is. What's the emergency? Who is the patient?"

"Sir, it would be better if I could just meet you there —"

"Not until I get a straight answer. Who is the patient? It will help me in my evaluation if I know now —"

"Sir, its your family. You wife, Marie, and your son, Daniel."

"Wh-Wh-What…happened? How could…" This made no sense, they weren't patients. Marie had mentioned that morning the two of them were going to Winstead's for hamburgers, then shopping at the Plaza. Thats where they were, now. Weren't they? What….how….?

"Sir, we can send a police car for you if you'd like —"

"Tell me, what's happened to them? Tell me now, dammit!"

"Uh…well, I'm so sorry to tell you this over the phone, but they were killed by a drunk driver on Ward Parkway. He swerved, hit the side of their car, and sent them into one of the big fountains and they were both killed instantly." Jeff would later find out their blood had flowed from the open car doors into the fountain, and that fountain had sprayed a pinkish color for the next forty-five minutes, causing traffic to slow down, as people stared.

Jeff couldn't talk or think. His golfing buddies to drove him to the hospital where he identified the shredded, reddish bodies of his pretty wife, Marie, 32, and his little son,

Tales from the Silver State IV

Daniel, 5, who had opted to wear his beloved Little League uniform.

The days and nights that passed, a surreal blur, the two funerals together, the dozens of people, the extra food, the offers to do what they can, anytime, just call, and the only time Jeff was fully present in the moment was to think: bring them back, just bring them back, and shove your chicken and walnut casserole. But he did not say that out loud, he suffered in his own silence, waiting until the large, dark dream house was empty, the dream having crashed into a pretty fountain. He awoke to more family, friends, well-wishers, and it was ten days before he was finally allowed some rest, some time to be alone, in the big new house that was supposed to house and nurture himself and Marie and Daniel and their future children, and someday, grandchildren.

Jeff, not knowing what day it was, had awoken in the empty, too-large house, only eight months since close of escrow. He put on an old shirt, jeans and sneakers, went downstairs, made the morning coffee, idly, and in idle himself, just going through the motions. The silence of the house was screaming at him, so he turned the TV on, but the news was that late-1960's video stew of Vietnam, campus riots, protests, cops beating up on kids, all things that were now ten million miles from his slightest interest. He turned off TV; the silence started yelling at him

Tales from the Silver State IV

So Jeff went out, sat out on the patio deck, alone, with his bad cup of coffee, since he kept misjudging how much to make for just one person. He stared off, hearing distant sounds of not-close neighbors, lawn mowers, kids playing, not his.

Jeff had loved his home, but now, it was now just a house. Worse, an empty mockery, a mausoleum of what was supposed to be, base camp for a future that to a left turn into being pink fountain water, with the two centers of his universe six feet beneath the moist April dirt of Kansas, maybe also in heaven.

Heaven.

Jeff wondered, with a depth of bitterness that permeated everything;
do I believe they are in heaven now? I guess I believe it. Jeff had been a routine Presbyterian who attended church, without passion. But cosmic questions came to mind now. He had believed in God, if ever asked, but, now, clearly, he decided, God did not believe in him. Well intentioned mourners said things like, they're in a better place, or that God has called them home, or, the worst one God moves in mysterious ways, his wonders to perform. That thought, he could not take. The deaths? Hardly a wonder.

God.

God, he thought. He finally focused on God. Jeff knew he believed in God, and actually had prayed, prior to a

Tales from the Silver State IV

local fountain performing God's miracle of turning regular water into light pink.

Wait. Believing in God, he realized, cuts both ways. If I believe in God, who knows everything and does everything, and I have sincerely prayed to thank him for the rich bounty of my life, then God is also responsible for this terrible, purposeful destruction. God was guilty of doing this to him, with malice aforethought. People said he should pray, but isn't praying just arguing with God about His will? Who is anyone to argue with God? God chose this accident to happen. The drunk driver, God's random instrument, was a family man, later to lose his license, do two-years in a minimum security prison, then be free to again enjoy again his wife, his children, his life. Jeff didn't even feel great anger at the driver, he was just some idiot, God's hammer in his tool box of choices, carefully selected to pound out all happiness and meaning of Jeff's life. God caused the pain Jeff was fully feeling and would feel forever. God did this to me.

It was a moment of instant clarity.

God did this to me.

Why me? he thought, aware of the absurdity of the cliche; no one asks 'why me?' when God gives them great blessings. Why little five-foot seven me, me, who people tell me with my short prematurely graying hair, and my first name, remind them a little of the old movie star, Jeff Chandler? Why me, who worked hard in medical school

then was lucky enough to win Marie? And then be blessed
with Daniel? Why me? Jeff knew he was no saint; there was
that blonde office temp last year, and Jeff rarely saw a reason
to confuse the I.R.S. with every tiny detail of his income, but
were those sins so evil God decided I deserved to lose my
family? One tacky affair and cheating on my taxes? God
destroys in mysterious ways, his pain to inflict.

Jeff sat on the patio deck, surrounded by woods, with
one small hill about sixty feet from the main house, open, no
trees around it, a place Jeff had promised Daniel he would
build a playhouse for him. He'd had every intention of
doing that too. Daniel was delighted, saying he would help.

Jeff knew that moment, more than ever, that one of
the biggest mistakes humans always made was assuming
'there's always time.'

No. Time is luck. Its that simple, he thought, and God
stole my luck.   But I can still build Daniel that
playhouse! That's when Jeff, his thoughts and feelings,
empty rafts in a churning inner sea of rage, decided he
would go ahead and build Daniel's playhouse now. Without
further reflection, he went to the garage, got the tall shovel,
deciding to make a beginning. He carried the shovel up to
the top of the little hill, and imagined Daniel there, in his
beloved Little League uniform (his whole team had to come
to his funeral, each five year old either giggling or crying,
depending.) Jeff imagined Daniel standing there, excited,
imagining the boy asking if he could help build the

playhouse, and Dad saying - I'm no longer anyone's father, Jeff realized suddenly - I'm not a Dad, and before he could dig one little chunk of earth for the pointless playhouse, he couldn't imagine Daniel there with him anymore; God had taken his Little League player out of the game, permanently benched, never to play again. Daniel, his whole wonderful, rich, good life ahead of him, now buried deep in that white child's coffin, because God decided it needed to happen. Jeff couldn't escape the obvious: God had done this. God had murdered his family.

Jeff collapsed, sobbing, leaning on the shovel, bending over, his grief, his open wound, finally exploding up out of him. He didn't know how much he'd been bottling up inside, but it was volcanic. Jeff heard someone sobbing loudly, yelling, then realized it was him. Jeff was then making noises like an animal, raw screams, from what was left of his soul. He heard himself yelling up at God, in total hatred, and he was on his feet now, cursing up at the sky, a light blue, nice day, scattered white puffy clouds. Jeff screamed up at God, and threw the shovel straight up in the air, as if to strike God with it, and the shovel spun and flew straight up, paused, tumbled down, landing twenty feet from Jeff, who ran to it, and threw it up again, angrily, screaming his hatred at God, using every curse word, ever ugly obscene expression he'd ever heard of, aiming them all at God. He kept throwing the shovel as high as he could, cursing, screaming, over and over, until he collapsed, exhausted, but still cursing God, a red scrape on his arm from the edge of the metal shovel.

After the neighbors called the police, Jeff spent three months in a local mental hospital. The first month he calmly articulated his hatred for God, to doctor after doctor, and how he wished God was man enough to come out, fight fair, not be sneaky and kill his wife and son. Jeff was clear and calm about wanting to hurt God, to kill him, to inflict pain on Him.

But by the end of the first month, Jeff realized he was not serving himself nor his new goal to try to somehow hurt God, by saying these things out loud. He was sane enough to know: it made no sense, what he wanted. There was no way to strike back at God, who knew everything; how do you sneak up on someone who has ESP? You can't ever get close enough.

Then Dr. Jeffrey Fields realized how he could someday maybe get close enough to God to do something to him. If it's not possible to kill God, and he realized it sort of wasn't, or even hurt him, could he at least spit in his eye? He'd do something to God someday, for this. And he just figured out how to get there, to get close to God. He laughed at the absurdity of the simplicity of his new scheme. He thought of it as the Plan. And while he knew God would see it coming, it was all he could think of to do, to at least try. So Jeff changed his tactics completely. He was a doctor, he knew what they wanted to hear. Jeff started by saying he knew he'd been saying terrible, senseless things, and that he was starting to come to his senses. He knew medical people needed scientific reasons to explain things to himself so he volunteered for any and all shock treatments and chemical experiments, and stuck to his story: that he now realized he'd had a mental breakdown, but it was over, he was himself again and just wanted to quietly go back to rebuilding a new life for himself. Jeff said he wanted to work as a doctor again, help people, and maybe be lucky enough to fall in love again, get married, raise a new family, believe in God, and have a good life.

They bought it.

He was released with follow-up counseling but Jeff quietly, never telling anyone, began to initiate his new lifelong Plan, by selling his house, while doing volunteer work at free clinics in the poorest part of town.

The Plan was simplicity itself: how could one ever get close enough to God to try to hurt him? By living the best possible life he could, the most Christian, unselfish life imaginable all his life, so he'd be able to go to heaven, meet God, and then have one good chance at him, just get me close enough, he thought, and I'll take my best shot at the arrogant destroyer. And I can do that on His own terms: live a completely good, unselfish life helping others! That's how to get to heaven and hurt Him!

So over the decades to come, Dr. Jeff Fields volunteered his time and medical training wherever it was needed, anywhere, globally, never taking anything for himself, living cheaply off the proceeds from the sale of his house and some stocks, but if he had to do without, he did without. He signed up at the Red Cross as a medical volunteer, for the rest of the 1960's, then the 1970's, was sent to relief camps in Africa, then to China after an earthquake, then to the slums of Rio de Janeiro. He suffered, caught diseases and did without any emotional or practical sustenance. He lived a Spartan life, doing anything he could to help others. People he worked with thought he was a saint. He gave away whatever he had, went without, always took the toughest cases, worked the longest hours. When opportunities for love or friendship came his way, he smoothly sidestepped them, since that would be selfish of him and he kept volunteering his medical training. A remote site for those with Hanson's disease in the Sudan, yet leprosy and God did not yet take him. He gave up a kidney for a teenager who would die without one in the Papua New Guinea. He helped sick people who survived digging into the huge landfill in Mexico City. Egypt. Bosnia. Doctors without borders. He worried only that Mother Teresa, aging symbol of unselfishness, was puling the same thing, and would get to stand before God before he had a chance, and somehow, hurt Him first; what God did to that bitch to get her to act so good, he idly wondered? He got older, and was no in great health himself, and continued to have no love, nothing, for himself. And no one could keep him from volunteering his time, any assets, or his medical help to Thailand sums, the poor sections of Liverpool, the endless refugee camps of Libya. It was a lifetime of service, truly, only for others.

He found himself, at age 86, in 2016, in a charity ward, in a London
hospital, dying. He thought lovingly of his long lost son, Daniel, always age 5, his beautiful wife, Marie, endlessly young, pretty, as the pain drugs took over. A hospital chaplain visited. Old Jeff prayed with him, but no one but Jeff, and probably God, knew what he was always really praying for: a chance at God. Then, one night, alone, no one holding his hand, a lifetime of unselfish accomplishments behind him, tubes up his nose, alone, he died.

Jeff woke up 38 years old again, feeling very good. He couldn't ever remember feeling this good inside. He was casually dressed, sitting on the deck of his old two-story house, only now it was by a beautiful lake, and on the nearby hill on his property, was a beautiful boy's playhouse. The sky, nearing sunset, offered beautiful unreal pastels. A winged white horse flew casually across the sky. Roses, twenty feet high, bloomed across the lake. Deer frolicked, unafraid. Jeff knew it his heart now, he'd made it. Heaven. He could feel it, he could feel goodness inside him.

Then he heard the patio glass door slide open behind him, and a very pleasant elderly short man with a smile and a twinkle in his eye sat down beside him, placing a cup of coffee for each on the table between them. The man looked like the actor Edmund Gwen who had played Santa Claus in MIRACLE ON 34th STREET. Wait, it was Edmund Gwen. Was it? He wore an expensive pinstriped grey suit, tie, a handkerchief the color a fountain water. Was this God, Jeff wondered.

"Yes, I am," God answered back, slight English accent. "I chose this form because its pleasant, but if you prefer, I can be a twelve-foot high man with a long white beard up on a throne. I am every God of every religion. Welcome to heaven. You wouldn't be here unless you'd earned my love for all of time."

Jeff studied him, amused, as he sipped his coffee, distracted by how warm and real he felt inside, a feeling a great goodness, without bitterness, or rage. Strange. "You know exactly how I like my coffee," Jeff said, never expecting this to be the first thing he'd say to God.

"Yes," God said, "but for me to know how you like your coffee is hardly an accomplishment after resurrecting a carpenter and watching every little sparrow fall. So, you're here, after a great deal of trouble, a selfless life of helping others, all so you can hurt me, is that right, my son?"

"You killed my wife and my son and ruined my life."

"Yes, I killed your wife and your son, long ago, it's true, I did. What you did with your life after that was your choice. That pesky free will thing."

"Why did you kill the two people I loved?"

Tales from the Silver State IV

"I don't mean to sound flippant, but that would be telling. And its that simple. I conduct tests, I have a master plan, lots of moving parts." God gestured: the sky briefly revealed the colorful Milky Way and a million stars, then faded back to the beautiful sunset, as God shrugged, sipped his coffee. "Explaining a single bolt on a 747 would not reveal it was a plane, where it was headed, or why. it would just explain a single tiny piece."

"Cut the bullshit chit-chat, you murderer. You killed my wife and son."

God sighed, then motioned to the evening sky. "Would you like to see a new color you didn't know existed?"

Jeff did not smile or react. God put down his coffee. "Jeff, my son, and you are my son, I do love you, I always have, you are now and forever fully in the presence of God's love for you...do you not notice as you speak those very words, that your lifelong rage and anger is no longer present inside you? Take a moment. Do you feel the same as you've felt since the day I took your family? Or even your tired old anger at me when you died?"

Jeff thought and said, "No, I don't. Its as if I am...just saying them now...out of habit....but you...you took my wife and son...why?" That was when Jeff began crying. God put his arm around him and pulled him close.

"Yes, my son, I did. You'll feel better soon, then forever. Such is the power of love." Jeff sobbed, his body shaking out the last of his bitterness and rage. "You're not the first to try your Plan, you know. Mother Teresa came at me with a broken tea cup, trying for my eyes. But she's in great peace now, working in her garden, not far from here."

"I don't understand anything," Jeff finally said, drying his eyes.

"You'll understand more soon, not everything. This is not a place of science or logic. It is about love. You thought you wanted revenge. But you really wanted redemption, from your rage, even that residual guilt we feel when someone dies but we get to live. And you have redemption now. You've earned it. Jeff, you will soon feel wonderful, love, and for forever."

But then Jeff asked, "If you knew all my Plan all along, and I really sort of knew that if you existed at all, you would know, why am I here? Why have you let me come to heaven where I wanted to hurt you, not love you?"

"Jeff, haven't you been aware you've been a little mentally ill with your Plan, all along?"

"Yeah, I sort of knew it didn't make any sense."

"Right, it made no sense. Do you feel mentally ill now? Or do you feel different?" Jeff nodded. God went on. "Do you think I turn away the sick, of mind or body? No. You are healed, and are slowly realizing it."

"But my life of volunteering to help others, that was just a ploy, so —"

Tales from the Silver State IV

"I knew that and you knew I knew it. But that also came from the part of you that was healthy and good. Beside, what we do matters so much more in life than what we think. And you did such great good for tens of thousands. All your life. You think that counts for nothing?"

Jeff just stared at him, confused. "But inside, I'm no good."

God sighed, and quietly said, "You thought your life was about revenge someday, against me. But it wasn't. You redeemed yourself through a lifetime of service to others. Thousands had better lives, because of you."

Jeff looked confused.

"I am right here," God's gentle voice continued. "Are you trying to hurt me now? Are you wanting to? Do you feel like you're crazy with hatred now?" God paused, and smiled. "Many experience bad and pass it on. You experienced bad and your behavior was to help others."

Jeff leaned back, looking out at the lake, reflecting the sunset's beauty, but real beauty he experienced was inside him now, growing.

"And for all your scheming how to get here, you forgot the two wonderful things about this afterlife."

"What two things?"

"My healing love, here, waiting for you, after your solitary life. And you forgot the other ways you won't ever feel alone."

Tales from the Silver State IV

Jeff didn't understand until he heard Daniel's voice, yelling, "Hey, Dad! Come see my great playhouse!"

Jeff slowly looked over and saw his son, Daniel, age 5, on the small hill, beside his terrific playhouse, and also, his beautiful, pretty young wife, Marie, standing there in a light yellow summer dress, smiling and waving, her brown hair blowing gently in the wind. Jeff was on his feet, and looked at God. Jeff sobbed out, "But I don't deserve this…this happiness. I don't."

"You do or you wouldn't be here." God said, gently. "No one has to be perfect. Even me, I keep forgetting how hard it is for people to forgive themselves. I'll have to work on that. You're a good man. Forgive yourself. Now go enjoy the love you have created."

Jeff ran to his family, and held them tightly, forever.

Tales from the Silver State IV

MANIFEST
By Susan Joslyn

His wife was killing him. It didn't matter, in the end, that she wasn't clever. So what if she couldn't devise an elaborate plot? He had made it easy for her. Now, she was starving him to death, and there was nothing he could do about it.

He tried telling people. Last week he mumbled at some visiting neighbors, "My wife is killing me." His relief at producing this cry for help evaporated as soon as he saw the looks on their faces. "It's the drugs talking," they reassured each other, patting his wife on the shoulder and giving *her* sympathetic looks. It was a twisted hunger strike, he thought, his wife was the one on strike while he was the one going hungry.

In earlier days, when people came to visit, he'd make his cute face and say he was hungry. With everyone watching, darling Elsie would make a show of fixing some "favorite" food of his. Everyone nodded approvingly. "Poor Irwin," they would say. "He's lucky to have you," they would say. In those days the terror was at bay, and the reality seemed far away. He was beloved, the center of attention. But the time between people's visits had grown long, his wife's attentions had all but vanished, and he had grown ever frailer. Even when someone did come by, they never understood his particular collection of grunts anymore. He sounded like every old man trapped in a hospital gown since the dawn of bed pans.

Although his body was surely failing, everything remained crystal clear in his mind. What does a man think about while he is slowly dying in his living room? More than anything, else, this one thought about riding his motorcycle. Yes, *his* motorcycle, despite the fact that his wife had already sold it. Oh, yes, he could see himself marching over to that scraggly-haired guy's house, saddling up and riding away. Leaving it all behind. He closed his eyes to feel the familiar thrumming beneath his seat. That little wiggle, testing his shifting foot and his brake foot, usually catching a boob-bump from the wife seated behind him in the process. He leaned back in the saddle – nope, no wife there, now. He'd be riding solo from here on out. No helmet, either. The wind could whip his hair and scald his eyeballs. Shifting into second gear he hunched down into the eye of calm over the gas tank. The dust pinged against the windshield as he popped through third and fourth gear. He opened it up on the long straight highway through the Mojave, his head nodding to the strains of Steppenwolf's "Born to be Wild". After a long, fast ride he swung around Mount Charleston, taking the curvier road with the finesse of a younger man. Finally, he motored sedately up his driveway to the front door and turned off the key. Home again in sudden echoing silence.

Later, awareness tugged at the edges of his mind when Elsie's little subcompact pulled into the garage vibrating the walls of the trailer. The engine switched off, and he listened for the car door. A long moment passed before he heard it. She probably dreaded coming in. She had a crappy job, still she made it clear that she'd rather be there than here. Hanging out with him was no picnic, he knew, even before get got sick. It had been bad ever since he lost his job and worse once he lost all hope of ever getting another one. She got a part-time, no-benefits job at the casino and spent most of her days there – sometimes for work. He didn't care. His days were spent slowly consuming that day's bottle along with whatever was on TV. When Elsie got home, she poured a drink from the orange juice bottle where she kept it mixed in the refrigerator and then she would join him on the couch. That would be their evening. If there was any conversation it might be her complaining bitterly about her job or berating his drunkenness which he would return with biting condemnation. There was no respect and less affection between them. He would have bet on loyalty. All the years and all the tears had burned them into one another.

Tales from the Silver State IV

Reality told a different story and so time crept by while his life ebbed away, not doing either of them any good.

The car door finally opened, then the garage door. He heard her heavy step in the kitchen and detected the aroma of a toasted deli sandwich. He could see the kitchen table where the nurse sat, the picture of calm, a magazine spread open before her.

"Evening," Elsie said.

"Hello, dear. How was your day?" The nurse had taken over as the "Hi honey I'm home" partner, although Irwin couldn't remember he and Elsie ever having such a polite conversation.

"Oh, long." Elsie's stock answer, he thought with disdain. He could tell her what a long day was like if she asked. But she wouldn't ask. She stepped in where he could see her now. He noticed the familiar way that she blew her hair out of her face; her hands still filled with her purse, keys, and the paper bag containing the sandwich.

"How is he?" Elsie asked the nurse, her voice lowered.

"No change." That same caring, hushed tone.

The nurse – what was her name? Carol. Or was it Karen? Did it matter? - gave his wife a report of their day.

Tales from the Silver State IV

She told a good story, considering that she had slept the day away on the couch in the other room. Except for when she spoke on the phone with her daughter, whom she was putting through college by working double shifts, and didn't hesitate to remind of that fact.

"Did you get him to eat something?" That was his wife's "super concerned" voice.

"No. He hardly made a move all day." *Like she would know.*

"I've picked up one of his favorite sandwiches," Elsie held up the bag.

"Smells good."

"Maybe that will entice him to eat it." Irwin pictured Elsie's smile, her dimples joining the blonde ringlets framing her round face to complete the deceptive image of a Botticelli angel.

As soon as she had seen the nurse out the door, Elsie grabbed her sandwich, stormed back to the second bedroom and closed the door. She didn't look Irwin's way; much less ask after his day. She'd be out later to give him morphine, he knew, but she probably assumed the nurse had given him his eight o'clock dose. She hadn't. The thought of staying awake and aware both thrilled and terrified him. Life is to be lived though, no matter how small that life became.

Muffled through the closed door, Irwin could hear Elsie booting up her computer and opening her paper deli bag. Then the inane chatter. He didn't know the male voice, but he knew that Elsie prattled endlessly to him every night, the poor soul. He couldn't discern all of the conversation, but he mentally filled in the blanks, like a demented game of Mad-Libs, inserting ridiculous words and phrases, cracking himself up.

The door clicked, and Elsie thumped down the hall to the kitchen. He heard the lid on the garbage can lift and the crumple of her sandwich wrapper, then the thud of her footsteps back down the hall to the bedroom.

Thinking of her dinner made his stomach clench and growl. Man, what he wouldn't give for a vanilla milkshake. Closing his eyes, he could taste the cold, creamy treat as it slid easily down his throat, coating his tightened belly. He could feel himself relax as he took another pull on the straw, then another. When he finished, he fell into a satisfied, non-narcotic sleep.

He heard her come in, muttering about the nurse not clearing up her drink cup. He kept his face a careful mask and she walked away without giving him morphine. He slatted his eyes to watch her full bottom swinging beneath the ratty T-shirt and his mind's eye followed her into their bedroom. Once upon a time their marriage had been filled with friends, motorcycles, beer and languid hours in that monstrous bed. Gradually the friends vanished – often because of the motorcycles and the beer – until they were left alone with their contemptuous familiarity. Their love-life flirted briefly with the endangered list, then moved quickly to extinction.

#

Sunday morning meant no nurse would be coming. Irwin woke to the sound of Elsie making breakfast, humming to herself. She seemed happy, free of his demands. Later, she bustled in with an armload of towels to fold using the dining room table. Irwin struggled to sit up on one elbow. He felt stronger this morning. No morphine for two days, plus the milkshake. As soon as that thought formed, he realized that it was nonsense. Of course he hadn't really had a milkshake.

Whatever miracle had given him the strength to pull himself up suddenly gave way, and he collapsed onto the pillows. This drew her attention, but only for a moment. He lifted himself up on one elbow again, eyed the stack of towels meaningfully and struggled for a word. "Bath."

"Don't be ridiculous." Her look was contemptuous before she turned back to her folding.

Tales from the Silver State IV

"Bath!" he demanded more firmly. Elsie jerked her head up, resentment flashing in her heavy-lidded eyes. Then her look became calculating.

"One last time," she muttered prayer-like under her breath. She left the room, returning with the small plastic tub, a new gown and a stack of clean sheets. He noticed that she also brought the morphine from the refrigerator. Gingerly peeling back the covers and removing his gown, Elsie swirled the washcloth in the warm water. She started at the top of his head. The cool air on his wet skin created a pleasant contrast with the warm washcloth. She moved it down the back of his neck and around to his chest.

Irwin closed his eyes and imagined a loving caress, not the business-like sponge bath. Her warm breath on his face as she reached across him to pull him to one side sent shivers down his spine. When her breasts brushed his chest, he found himself responding. He reached to place his hand on her back causing her to draw back and look into his face, her emerald eyes still beautiful if you ignored the life-weary face that housed them. He felt a tingling between them and remembered when he was a dashing Navy man, tall and straight in his uniform and she, the sixties flower child, a leather band around her head. The heat shimmered between them in those days. His body responded more fully to that memory, and Elsie noticed. A coy smile seemed to escape against her will. Ah, those dimples. He had forgotten how adorable she could be when she smiled. Unable to resist, he returned her smile with a mischievous grin and felt the years fade away. Their gazes locked, both caught in the phantom of passions they used to share. Elsie lowered her head, trance-like, and kissed his lips. Irwin growled and when he lifted her T-shirt over her head, all signs of weakness were gone, his movements sure. Her breasts swung loosely and he smiled at the memory of her bra-burning days when she declared that the girls would never go back to that tight prison. He felt the same way about cars, once he got the motorcycle. His arms tightened in remembered comraderie, and before either of them knew it Elsie's naked body moved astride him. They were cocooned in two simultaneous moments: the present, mild and familiar but also the past, an entrancing fantasy that wrapped them both in its hotter passion, driving a response from them that neither expected.

When it was over, she rested on the bed with him. Neither spoke. After a few minutes, she got up and hurried to pull her clothes back on without meeting his eyes. She retrieved the discarded washcloth and padded into the kitchen for more warm water then finished bathing him in the same business-like manner as before. She made the bed with the clean sheets, moving him to accommodate the effort and then replaced his gown and covered him in silence. Her gaze rested on him for an extra moment, her face blank.

Then she picked up the tub hurried out forgetting to give him the morphine again.

A sharp exclamation and a burst of cool air from outside startled him awake the next time. Elsie stood in the living room with the door open to the front porch. A breeze wafted in bringing dust and desert stickers with it. That usually made her crazy, but she didn't even appear to notice, this time, frozen at the door, staring at the porch. She turned to look at him, confusion and the beginning of anger twisting her face. Patience was an unfamiliar quality for him, but there was nothing like being trapped in a body that will hardly move to teach it to you. He waited.

"Ok, how did your motorcycle end up on the porch?" she finally demanded.

He just looked back at her, no expression on his skeletal features.

"I'm calling Fred. I hope he doesn't think I'm giving him his money back!"

Elsie marched through to the kitchen, and he could hear her rummaging for her phone and placing the call. She spoke; then she waited. After a few minutes, she returned to the living room eyes ablaze, shoulders up. He knew that fighting stance. "What's going on?"

Tales from the Silver State IV

Irwin returned her gaze in continued silence.

"Fred says he reported the bike stolen yesterday." Accusatory.

His mind began to whir.

"What did you do?" Strident, then incredulous. "How could you do *anything*?" She strode over to the front door again, perhaps expecting the motorcycle to have disappeared. But there it stood, shiny and beautiful.

"Where is your phone?" They both looked at the bedside table where it sat on the charger, far out of his reach. Elsie had been intercepting his dwindling calls for weeks, now. Her eyes narrowed as she looked at it doubtfully.

His thoughts were in chaos. Had he ridden the bike yesterday? What about the milkshake? Did they make love? Could he do those things again? *Was he going to live?*

Elsie clearly had the same thought, the fear blanched her features.

A satisfaction began to bloom inside him. It was the first time the cold, gnawing fear had abated in as long as he could remember. His wife's mouth was open but no words came out. A red flush spread across all visible skin.

Tales from the Silver State IV

"Look, one, you couldn't have ridden it." She held up one finger, and then added a second. "Two, you couldn't have called someone to ride it over here." She raised another finger. "So how, how did the bike get on the porch? Tell me!"

He lifted a mocking eyebrow. He was in control, again. She would have to answer for the way she treated him if he got well, wouldn't she?

"You could *not* have ridden it. You can't *ride a motorcycle!* You can't do *anything!*" She repeated, winding herself up to a high-pitched screech.

"You did say that, before." Maddeningly smug. His look turned knowing. "But … I can certainly do *some things*, can't I?" His large, watery blue eyes bore into hers, forcing her to remember. She blushed and looked away. Then turned and stomped from the room.

Irwin's mind struggled to adapt to the new reality. When he thought about how much he wanted to ride his motorcycle, he had actually done so. It had given him joy. When he thought about how much he wanted a milkshake, he had one. It had given him strength. After remembering the aching joy of making love to his wife in years past, he had unexpectedly done so, once again. It had given him succor. Hours earlier he could barely lift his head, yet with nothing but a memory he had, he could say, risen to the occasion. Three wonderful, impossible things had happened and he had enjoyed each one immensely. Could it continue? Could he manifest whatever he desired, just by thinking about how much he wanted it? Or was it all a morphine-fueled dream? Or … the thought dawned on him, had he already died? No, he discounted it immediately. This was like heaven and he doubted that's where he'd be.

Another test, he decided. He'd take the bike out and get a big juicy hamburger. Not chicken soup like a sick person. A disgustingly greasy, cholesterol-laden indulgence that he would feel well enough to sit up and enjoy. He closed his eyes and imagined riding again. Sure enough, he could feel the hot sun on his bare arms. He never rode with bare arms – but it felt so free! He spied the drive-through ahead and pulled in. He ordered the hamburger, clasped the folded top of the bag in his teeth and let the bike have its head on the way back, the thrill washing over him with the hot wind. Back in bed without any recollection of getting there, he had the hamburger on its opened wrapper on the tray table before him. He imagined the way it would taste, the greasy cheese, spicy peppers, the bread soft and warm, the pickles making a salty crunch. Popping the last bite into his mouth he laid back down, worn but pleased. He purposefully left the wrapper sitting on his tray table and closed his eyes to remember the ride and savor the lingering flavors. He couldn't wait to see what Elsie had to say.

Tales from the Silver State IV

When next he opened his eyes, Elsie sat on the edge of the bed looking at him. She was waiting for him to wake up and immediately pounced.

"Where'd you get the hamburger?"

He smiled. Yes! He was doing things that he thought he would never do again. He wasn't just going to live; he was going to live like a king!

"Who is coming over here and helping you?"

He didn't have an answer, and he didn't try to make one up.

"Figures. You always thought you could have whatever you wanted." There was the familiar resentment. He couldn't blame her. Yes, he could.

"I can have … whatever I want …" The words came out slowly, his voice weak but filled with wonder.

"Well, you can't make yourself well, can you?" Elsie demanded, showing a little smugness herself.

"What if I can?"

The punch landed soundly; she stepped back and her face crumpled. She *believed* that he was doing these things, and she *believed that he could get well*! Instead of quietly dying, starving in his own filth while she let it happen he would live and he wouldn't want for anything. She had bet that karma wasn't on his side. He could feel his anger rising, and he knew that she could see it, too. Karma wasn't just on his side, it was in his hands. His eyes closed in satisfaction.

He opened his eyes when he heard small sounds in the room. He eyed Elsie suspiciously as she slithered around the room with a dust cloth. He didn't speak, but not because he couldn't. When Susie-Homemaker had every surface wiped clean, she turned to him.

"Want to do it again?"

"What, the sex?"

"No," she averted her gaze then returned it to meet his. "Make something appear."

Irwin was silent. He was not going to do anything – not one thing – that *she* told him to do. Why would he?

"Leave me alone." He felt good. In command. Hopeful. Things he had not felt for some time. He closed his eyes again and this time he didn't open them until morning when he heard Elsie on the phone. She was calling her workplace. It was Monday, a work day, but she said her husband had taken a turn, and she needed to be with him. She also called the nurse agency and gave Carol the day off using the same story. When she passed by the living room door, he could see that she was freshly showered and wearing a sundress. The sundress wasn't a great look for her, but she had put in some effort. He heard her clanging around and then detected the unmistakable smell of bacon and eggs. He loved bacon and eggs. She brought it in on a tray. She hadn't as much as offered him an old French fry in days, but now she was fixing him a farmhand's breakfast. She set it up on his bedside tray and sat down to face him.

He looked at the food but found it didn't interest him. Betrayal was like a knot in his stomach. Her kindness always came with a price. She could not be trusted in his time of need.

"Make something appear." No preamble.

"Go to hell." It was like old times.

"Come on, Irwin. What else can you make appear? Can you make money?"

Silence.

"Try it," She cajoled.

Irwin wanted to try it, but he didn't want Elsie to get the money. The one thing he wanted most, he didn't have to share with Elsie: his health. If he were well, he wouldn't have to share anything with her, ever again.

Tales from the Silver State IV

"Irwin, make money. We can get anything we need." Elsie was still haranguing him.

He pursed his lips, trying to focus on being well. He didn't know how. He tried to think.

"Irwin!" His eyes snapped open in frustration. He needed to block her out. He imagined silence. How peaceful it would be if she would just go away. Her unwillingness to care for him unless there was something in it for her disgusted him. He needed for her to go away along with that annoying disembodied voice that she chatted with each evening. Plus, if she were gone, all of her crowd of décor items that looked like chickens would be gone, too. He hated those chickens. He'd replace them with a few Eagles. He liked Eagles. He closed his eyes to picture it. When he opened his eyes, he was alone. The kitchen looked different, bare. The brass salt and pepper shakers on the table were a pair of Eagles. He didn't see or hear Elsie. His closed his eyes to stop the pounding in his head.

#

On Tuesday, when Carol showed up for work she wondered about the big Harley Davidson motorcycle parked on the front porch. She knocked on the door and waited. When she heard no reply, she tried the doorknob and found it unlocked. Irwin's stick-thin figure was on the bed, but there was a different stillness about him. She stepped over and felt his arm. Cold. He was gone. She looked through the house for Elsie and found no sign of her. Opening the garage door, she saw that the little hatchback there. She wandered through the house, cautiously tapping on and then opening the door to the small second bedroom. There had been a lot of stuff in this room – papers, a computer; it was empty now. She checked the master bedroom. She didn't remember the soaring brass Eagle mounted to the wall over the bed. There was no sign of Elsie.

Tales from the Silver State IV

THE KNIFE

By Danét Palmer

It was the first time I would see the children since the State had stepped in; since they were sent to live with their father a hundred miles away. I had to get a rental to pick them up because my car was in the shop.

Would they want to come back with me? Would they hate me for what happened? Would they ever trust me again? These were the thoughts that kept me company on the long drive from Las Vegas to Utah.

Jessie and Nick were waiting on the front porch of their father's house; Jessie, with her little pink suitcase and Nick, his spongebob backpack. I felt lightheaded as I pulled into the driveway. Opening the door, I stepped out cautiously. The children matched my pace, standing up slowly, picking up their bags.

Nicholas finally broke the spell. He ran and jumped up on me saying, "Mom, you're here!" Jessie's arms circled my waist with more reserve. But as we drove away, I took my first real breath, and hoped that I would *keep* breathing.

When we went together to pick up my car at the shop the next day, however, there was a big surprise. Parked in front of the station was an unmistakably familiar car; one that belonged to the man who had been the reason I lost my children in the first place.

Holy shit! Rick is here? "Breathe," I told myself. *He probably just dropped his BMW off for servicing. You're just going to be in and out. This can be simple.*

I told the kids to wait outside, hoping they wouldn't see him. While settling my account and returning the rental, I was doing fine. Until I saw Rick talking to the mechanic, walking slowly out from the garage.

Suddenly, little Nicholas bolted past me! I grabbed him by the arm. "Where are you going?" I cried.

"Just want to see somethin'," he said. At three, he was just getting the hang of complete sentences. "If Rick's here."

Fuck. How do I handle this?

I knelt down and looked at Nick, eye to eye. "Yes, sweetheart. Rick is here. But, I don't—"

"Jus' want to tell him somethin'."

Tales from the Silver State IV

Could I let him speak with his abuser? Did I have the right to refuse him? God, I wished my heart would slow, let me catch my breath.

"I don't know, honey," I said.

"But I just wanna tell him somethin,"

"Ok, honey, but take my hand. We'll 'tell' him together." As we walked into the garage, Nick's little hand squeezed mine as I told him not to step in the grease puddles that carpeted the floor of the garage.

That's when he saw us. Seeing Rick's face brought all the events of the last two years flooding into my mind.

****

I met him at a private party at Caesars Palace. This was a big deal for me, my first invitation to mingle with "who's who" in Vegas. I was thrilled to be the guest of a celebrity, a headline impersonator at the Golden Nugget. It was the kind of invitation that says, "Yes, you've made it. You're in. You're somebody."

Dressed to impress, in a red sequined mini—and cocaine confidence—I made the rounds feeling lively and beautiful. The men, with expensive suits and _____ manicured hands, were men of power and influence. Some were entertainers or models that I recognized from billboards. They were gorgeous, confident, and they all seemed to say, "If you don't know who I am, you want to."

The currency was admiration, esteem, and awe, and it flowed like the fountain in the center of the room. It made me feel giddy and alive.

When I spotted Rick playing blackjack with a small cluster of women gathered round him, attentive and enamored, I could relate. There was something about his presence that drew me in, yet I tried to remain aloof. Eventually, I made my way past him with a hint of flirtation.

Smiling, he reached out and touched my arm as I walked by, What are you drinking?" He asked as he waved a waiter over with the flick of his hand. "I'm Rick Thompson – Rick's Salons & Spas? What's your name?"

I was familiar with the spas. Who wasn't? "Char," I replied, and he motioned for the others to make room for me. "Scotch," I said, sliding in next to him.

He played a few more hands before he said, "Let's get out of here; go somewhere where we can hear ourselves think." His voice was deep, soothing, and seductive. I felt heady. *With dozens of beautiful women to choose from, he was picking me?* But I fell into his confident stride, and tucked myself comfortably beneath his broad shoulders and lean physique. I was the bell of the ball, picked by the prince.

We drove up to Red Rocks, looking out over the city of Vegas lights. Sitting in his convertible, the cool breeze and refreshing conversation, were the perfect night cap for this hot Vegas night. I was impressed that he didn't ask me to come to his place, let alone want to sleep with him. When he dropped me at my home, he drew me into his arms, lightly brushing his lips on mine, and whispered, "Till, the next time," and opened my door.

The next day, returning home from one of my psychology classes at UNLV, I received a single red rose. The card said, 'Simply beautiful.' It spoke to me of respect and value – the epitome of romance.

"What a class act," I thought.

But a week passed and I didn't hear from him. Three weeks and a day passed and still he didn't call.

Then one day, there was a knock at my door. I answered it, and there he was. This time he had two red roses. "Couldn't stay away any longer," he said with a slight smile.

"Thank god the kids are with their dad this weekend," I thought to myself.

Tales from the Silver State IV

Rick walked around my living room, inspecting it. "Now come," he said. I have something to show you."

I had a pharmacology class in an hour, but I knew I couldn't refuse him.

We drove in his black BMW convertible, top down, to Marché Bacchus, a little French restaurant set on a lake. I'd heard about it. It was considered one of the most elegant restaurants in Vegas. As we pulled up, the valet said, "Hello, Mr. Thompson. Hope you enjoy your evening." The maître d' too seemed to know Rick, and he seated us on the patio overlooking lake Jacqueline. I was overwhelmed with the twinkling lights, like little stars glittering on the surface of the water. Swans glided past us, hardly making a ripple in the still reflection.

I learned that Rick was a wine connoisseur. He taught me to look at the color, the opacity and viscosity, to first smell, then to taste. He taught me to let the tongue take in the subtle bouquet of the wine; then to notice the slight change in aroma as I swallowed it. He tested me with each step. I tried to please him with every answer. There was a slight nod of approval when I got it right. He looked away when I didn't. I was learning the language of relationship with Rick.

That night, as he kissed me at my door, I still wasn't sure if I'd ever see him again. I wanted to. I was captivated. Being with Rick meant being a part of the elite, the 'real' people in Vegas.

One week to the day, he called for me again. I hustled to get someone to cover my shift at the Chinese restaurant and asked daycare to keep the kids for the night. I was just changing when the doorbell rang. I opened the door and asked him to sit and make himself at home. "I'll just be another minute," I said.

When I returned, he was standing right where I left him. Stiff.

"What's wrong?" I asked.

He looked down at his watch. "Priorities. Be ready when I come for you."

"I'm sorry," I said softly. "It won't happen again."

His face changed instantly from disapproving to charismatic. Putting his arm around me, he said, "We're going to swing by my place. Consider yourself special."

I felt special. I was being invited to his private domain, which I imagined to be an invitation to his heart as well.

As we pulled into the circular drive of his large Spanish Colonial home, I was impressed. It was immaculate, clinically clean. Every surface clear except the occasional black and white sculpture of naked bodies intertwined, or a sleek and stunning lamp on a sofa table. It was a study in contrasts: white walls with black and white photo art. White carpet, black sofa. Black and white stainless steel kitchen. Black linens on the bed, and black towels in the bath. A single black rose in a white bud vase on the bathroom counter.

I felt Rick watching me as I took in the decor. Then drawing me into his arms, he kissed me softly. I felt intimidated, intoxicated. I pulled him toward the bed but he stopped me, placing his finger on my lips and said, "Time to go."

And that was it. That was the whole date. He took me home and said, "Next week. And remember what we talked about."

What had we talked about? Being ready when he got there?

The night he finally brought me to his bed, he whispered, "Keep your eyes closed. Feel, rather than look. That's how you'll come to know me."

I did. He kissed me slowly, deliberately, tracing my neck with his lips, working his way down with lingering but unnerving gratification, and finally lifting me into his arms. I gave myself to his rhythm. And as the energy in my body rose, breath quickening, he brought me close to the edge, and then laid me back, tantalizingly out of reach. I was used to being in control with men; pacing them, bringing them to climax, not the other way around.

But I was in another world now, just learning its rules and pleasures.

****

Shaking my head, I brought my mind back to the moment. With a slight jerk of his chin, Rick mouthed to me, *"What the fuck are you doing?"*

I straightened my posture, hoping I looked stronger than I felt. "Nick wants to tell you something," I said.

Rick put a good face on it. "Hey, buddy, whatcha been doing?" he said, scrunching down to Nicholas's height.

Nick looked him in the eye, his tiny shoulders squared, and answered. "We've been to the fair," and slowly he pulled a little plastic knife out of his pocket, which he'd chosen as a prize from one of the games. "I got a knife," he said.

I caught my breath, feeling unsteady; the memories resurfacing of how I'd lost control of my life, becoming obsessed with Rick, comparing him to the artlessness of former lovers, measuring us against other couples; imagining ours was a relationship everyone might envy.

Tales from the Silver State IV

Sometimes he disappeared from my life for days or even weeks. No warning, no explanation. I didn't ask where he'd been though. I learned early what to ask and what to keep to myself. In his absence I could feel the danger of not measuring up, the fear of never being able to earn his love. A silent desperation would arise within me, a loneliness I'd never know before. Then he'd call or send flowers, and I'd slip back into my dream-state, wrapping my fears in a box and slipping them under the bed.

He watched me for slip-ups in my behavior and reprimanded me. "Is that the way you want me to think of you? Someone who doesn't wash her face before bed?" Or, "That camisole you have under your suit, isn't that something you wear only with your lover, with me? Act with class, Char."

One morning after showering, he called to me and I left my towel on the floor. Later, as he walked past me to the bathroom, he said, "Come here. Is this the way you treat my hospitality? Is this how little you think of me? You ungrateful little cunt!" And he shoved me to the floor. "There's water everywhere, you little bitch. Did you want me to slip?"

I looked up at him in shock, tears springing to my eyes. "No. I'm sorry. I was—"

Tales from the Silver State IV

"I don't want to hear your lame excuses. If you cared, you wouldn't have done this. Now clean it up!"

Even though he had never said it, I could tell Rick didn't like kids. So I knew I needed to keep my life with him separate from my life as a mother. During spring break, while the kids were with their father for a week, he asked me to stay with him, and we laid awake for hours, talking.

Well, he talked. I listened. He even talked about children, a subject we had always avoided. *Why is he bringing up kids? Does he want to get to know mine? Or is he saying I'm not a good mother?*

He said that children needed to be trained to do what adults tell them to do without questioning; that most parents were too lenient, with their kids growing up disrespectful and irreverent. *Was he talking about my children? Had he watched my parenting style with my kids? Yet he'd only seen us together a few times.* He told me how his father, a Navy Colonel, raised him to tow the line, ruling with fear and punishment, teaching him to suck it up and take it like a man.

One day, he said, "I need a favor. Tomorrow I go to court and I'd like you to be a character witness for me. Can you do that, baby? Will you? I need you right now."

How I had longed for him to call me an affectionate name

like, 'baby', to say he needed me, wanted me. "Sure, if you think it will help. I'll be there. I'll go with you."

As I waited outside the courtroom to be called in, an attorney from the other side approached me, asking me who I was with.

"Rick Thompson," I replied. "He's asked me to be a character witness."

The attorney said, "Do you have children? Because if you had seen the pictures and X-rays of that little girl, you'd get them as far away from this guy as you could. He nearly killed her." He pulled the photos from his portfolio. I glanced horrified, grabbed my purse and ran, stopping only when I got outside to catch my breath, my mind racing.

"What would I say when Rick asked me what happened? Could I just avoid him? Will he come after me? Or maybe there is an explanation. Then what? I'm the one that abandoned him in his time of need. Who am I?" And I went back in.

The attorney was gone. I waited in the hall, but they never called for me. When the session broke up, Rick came out. "They wouldn't let me have a character witness," he said. "The whole thing was a set-up to get a hefty settlement out of me. I'll pay. I'm just glad it's over. Thanks for coming."

Something changed in our relationship after that. Rick was

more vulnerable, but also more volatile. He began accusing me of sleeping with guys I met at work. He pushed me when he didn't think I was giving him my full attention. But then he'd send flowers or love letters, apologizing and saying he loved me.

I tried to understand, forgive, believe.

Then one day, he stuck me for not folding the bathroom towels correctly. Then just as quickly, he apologized, telling me it was pressure from work. I forgave him. Again.

One evening I had an important presentation for my clinical psych class. It was my final, and half the credit for the class. *I had to go.* My babysitter was a no show. I tried to reach her, to no avail. I tried getting two other sitters. Nothing. Rick called, and in a panic, I spilled out my dilemma.

"Bring them over here. You can put them down before you leave. They'll be fine," Rick said.

"Thank you," I said, resisting the apprehension rising in my heart. Yet I drove them to his house and put them to sleep in his bed, rushing off to class.

I hurried through my presentation and left as quickly as possible. Even so, the strip was a car to car gridlock. I panicked and finally got off on a side road. When I opened the door, Rick was sitting on the couch waiting for me. He patted the place next to him, telling me to sit down. I did.

"Nicholas, got up to use the bathroom," he said. "I was running a hot bath for you for when you got back. I told him to wash his hands. He put them down in the bath. I heard him scream. So I ran in and grabbed him. I put burn cream on his hands and gave him a cold wash cloth to hold while he went to sleep."

I got up, but Rick pulled me back down. "Let them get a little more sleep before you move them," he said. "Sit here with me and watch the news."

I sat there paralyzed. Still I didn't dare get up. We sat together, neither of us speaking, until he started to nod off. Eventually, his breathing slowed, and I knew he would soon be asleep. I waited. When I heard the first gentle snore, I slipped away and went in to the children. They were asleep.

When I saw Nicholas' hands, my heart shattered. They were blistered, the fingers stuck together. The skin was coming off where he'd been holding the wash cloth.

Everything went black, my whole world collapsing in on me. An Unimaginable horror crept over me. *What had I been thinking? How could I have left my children with a man that I, myself, was afraid of? A man I knew had issues with children? What kind of mother would do that?*

Tales from the Silver State IV

I woke up Jessica, shushing her, and gingerly lifted Nicholas into my arms. Then Rick appeared in the door.

"What's going on in here?" he asked.

"I'm taking him to the emergency room," I blurted out. "Right now." Pushing past him, I didn't know how I was doing it, but I kept moving. I was on autopilot.

At the hospital, they asked me what had happened. I told them what Rick had told me. They asked again. They said they thought I was covering for my boyfriend.

I told them that I only knew what Rick had said. I was grief stricken, ashamed, and guilty. I screamed, "Why do you keep asking me to say it again and again? I told you everything I know!"

The counselor took my hand. "We asked, because the extent of the burns indicate that his hands were held deliberately under extremely hot water, for an extensive period of time."

In shock I cried pitifully, "I thought they'd sleep and I'd be right back. I don't know what I was thinking! I knew better." Then the story about the court case spilled out of me. I told her that I had never left the children alone with him before and if it hadn't been an emergency— *Lame. Irrelevant. Couldn't the floor just open up and swallow me into hell, where I belonged?*

Tales from the Silver State IV

The counselor left and returned with two officers and a social worker. She said, "Because of your relationship with this man, we're taking your children. We can't trust you to keep them safe."

I couldn't breathe. *Of course she was right. I didn't deserve to be a mom. I didn't deserve to live.*

Even in my confusion, I remembered Gary, their father; I asked if the children could live with him. We called him, explaining the situation and he said he was on his way. A few minutes later they brought the children back to me. Nicholas' hands looked like gauze boxing gloves. I sat him on my lap, with Jessica next to me, and wept.

"I'm so sorry. I love you. I never meant for this to happen."

"It's ok, mom," they both kept saying. *Christ. They were taking care of me!* I didn't deserve it. I held on to them until their father arrived. He wouldn't look at me. He just knelt down and told the children they'd be staying with him for a while and that it would be ok. I placed Nick in his arms, Jessie took his hand, and without looking back they walked away.

That morning, driving away from the hospital, I vowed that I would do whatever it took to become someone worthy to see my children again. To become someone they could be proud of – someone they could forgive. I joined a domestic violence group and started therapy. I tried to forgive. But I couldn't forget. I tried.

The counselor had told me that the ultimate sign of healing is forgiveness. *Forgiveness? How do you forgive the unforgivable?*

I thought of the childhood that had made Rick so wounded. I thought of my own childhood and my despair in attempting to gain my father's love. I worked hard in therapy, uncovering the past, changing patterns that were revealed. Yet no justification story about Rick's childhood or mine, nor understanding the toxic, addictive pull that passed for love in our relationship, helped. How could I ever really forgive myself? Shouldn't guilt be a life sentence; a penance for this mother's sin? Forgiveness alluded me.

*****

Now, as Nick squeezed my hand, my mind returned to the present once again. His hands had healed over with just a trace of a scar where the skin had pulled off.

There he stood, brandishing his little knife before him. *What did it mean, this act of bravery? Was he saying, "You can't hurt us anymore – I'm not afraid of you?"*

Slowly he slipped the knife back into his pocket, still looking at Rick eye to eye. As Rick made to go, Nicholas put his hand on Rick's knee, and said, "Rick, I know you're sorry from burnin' my hands." – Changing everything.

Rick, speechless, stood up and walked away.

In awe I looked into my son's face, feeling a shift deep down. I let out a long slow breath. Hugging Nicholas, I felt his great big heart beating in sync with my own. And I realized I didn't know anything before that day, nothing that was true. I thought guilt was the price one paid for redemption. After all, guilt and shame were as much a part of me as my blonde hair and steel blue eyes.

But watching this scene with my little boy, knife in hand, courage expanding his little chest, standing up to Rick— the one thing I never did, could never do the entire time we were together—I saw through new eyes.

I felt the prison walls around my heart begin to crumble. Breathing, I felt my heart expand, and I let go, and let forgiveness happen. And in an instant of timelessness, I forgave myself.

I simply let go of wanting it to have been different. I let go of the shame, the penance, the need for justice, and let forgiveness move through me, accepting myself, just as I was.

That moment with Nicholas, I learned everything about forgiveness. Served up to me on the silver blade of a child's plastic knife. And a new life began.

Tales from the Silver State IV

MIRANDA'S REDEMPTION

By Marshall Prescott

"What do you mean by that? I've never even looked at your boyfriend, funny." Miranda said using air quotes.

"Yes you have! I've seen the way you look at him. You're drooling over him because your beau dumped you for some bimbo. Susan mimicked Miranda's quotes and rolled her eyes before she stomped off.

The tension was thick between the sisters, and a little more than normal. Susan was fed up with her sibling; she made absolutely no sense lately. They had been so close when they were younger, but now, Miranda's boyfriend had dumped her for a large busted blonde with absolutely no personality, causing a complete change in Miranda's and Susan's relationship. Now things had become heated, and for what, a boy named Luke?

"I don't care about your boyfriend." Miranda said standing in the doorway.

"Oh yeah, I've seen the way you look at him," Susan said rolling her eyes again.

Miranda made a face behind her sister's back when she wasn't looking. Then she walked away to end this stupid argument. There was no reason to continue.

Tales from the Silver State IV

☺☺☺

Susan plopped down on the bed and sighed with contempt. She was serious about Luke, at least more so than she had been with anyone else up to this point. Susan had wanted Luke for years, but six months ago, he actually showed interest in her so she made the move throwing herself at Luke, making sure he knew just how much she wanted him. Her mother thought she was infatuated with Luke, but she thought it was the big L, love. When they were at football games Susan was watching Luke, the was the perfect boy could do no wrong.

☺☺☺

As for Luke, he felt entirely different than Susan did. Whenever she wasn't around, every girl he past caught his eye, blonde, brunette, or even redhead, it didn't matter. Luke thought every girl wanted him, no, needed him. Luke thought every gal in school admired him for his blonde hair, blue eyes, and muscular physique.

Luke and Susan started having sex by the third or fourth date. Luke thought that was awesome. He'd keep her until someone better came along. Susan was completely devoted to him and that kept the relationship functioning.

☺☺☺

Susan thought that Miranda was flirting with Luke in an effort to take him away from her. But actually it was far from the truth. Luke flirted with Miranda when Susan wasn't looking. Miranda was wishing that Susan would catch Luke's wandering eyes, and see him flirting with other girls. The down side to that was her sister would be devastated. She would be absolutely crushed to witness Luke flirt with girls behind her back.

Miranda had dreams of leaving this small incompetent town for a bigger and larger metropolitan community. She had aspirations of becoming a veterinarian; she loved animals even more than human beings. Animals don't lie, you know exactly what they like or don't like. They show you all the time. Just watch them, that's all you need to do. They either love you or not. There is no hearing them say one thing, and do another, then have to figure it out. Animals are awesome friends.

Miranda wanted to help her sister understand what was going on, but Susan kept blaming Miranda for flirting with Luke. What could she do that would get Susan to see Luke carrying on with another gal. As hurtful as it would be for Susan, Miranda wanted Susan to see it, so she would stop blaming her for any disloyalty or infidelity.

Then, an awesome idea hit Miranda, solving the problem. She could do it, too. Miranda could bring Susan to the game after Luke was already there. If Luke had no idea that Susan was present he'd be himself, meaning that he would be flirting and carrying on with the other gals, and Susan would see him in action forcing her to realize that it was not Miranda that was the problem. Perfect! All Miranda had to do was get Susan to the game, but not let her notify

Tales from the Silver State IV

Luke that she was coming. Miranda could make sure she borrowed the car for a meeting with the debate club, when she returned to the house, she could pick up Susan and take her to the game. The only bug in the ointment was the phone. Miranda would have to keep Susan from texting Luke. She'd have to ponder on that. This plan may not be as good as it originally sounded, but it seemed to be the only plan so far.

On Sunday while Luke was at the house seeing Susan, Miranda overheard Luke tell Susan that he couldn't take her to the game on Friday because his truck would be in the shop for brake repairs. He would pick up the truck right after the game.

Miranda talked with her mom making sure that she had use of the family station wagon on Friday to attend a club meeting. It worked; mother agreed the car was hers Friday after school. Now, the only problem that remained was the cell phone issue.

Then it came to Miranda she could brush past Susan carrying a soda, spilling some on Susan. When Susan goes to clean up and change clothes, Miranda could take the phone and offer to drive her to the game as an apology for the incident. If Susan said anything about not having a phone, Miranda would offer to allow Susan use of her phone on the drive to the game, but she would not bring it. That would prevent Susan from warning Luke she was coming. Miranda sighed. It was a pretty good plan and she was hopeful she could pull it off. Now, Miranda could hardly wait.

When Friday came, Miranda was sure to mention that she would need the car to meet with the debate team right after school. Susan rolled her eyes as she put her breakfast bowl in the sink.

When Miranda got home from school she busied herself about the house getting ready to go, waiting for the perfect opportunity to spill on Susan. Finally, her chance came. Miranda grabbed the glass of soda, walking fast, she went by Susan, tripping as she past, spilling cola on Susan's blouse.

"Hey, watch it," Susan said. "Look what you did!"

"Oh no, I'm sorry Susan. I…" Miranda was cut off by Susan.

"You could have been more careful, you know. Damn. I have to get this out," Susan said as she stomped into the bathroom.

Miranda put the glass in the kitchen sink, then went into the bedroom and searched for Susan's cell phone. Not seeing it anywhere in sight, Miranda took her phone out of her pocket and stared at it, contemplating whether she should call her sister's phone. It could be in her pocket, but it could be somewhere else as well. What should she do? Susan would be out of the bathroom soon and Miranda needed to have Susan's phone to prevent her from spoiling the surprise or everything she had done was for nothing.

Tales from the Silver State IV

Where could the phone be? Desperate, she dialed Sue's number.

It rang twice before Susan said, "What do you want now, isn't it enough you ruined my shirt? What's your problem?" Susan said.

Miranda thought fast before replying. "I just wanted to say I'm sorry. I feel bad, but it was an accident." Miranda's heart sank knowing that Susan had her phone with her. How could she get that phone away from her?

Imitating her voice from younger years, Miranda said, "Suzzy, can you ever forgive me?" Miranda stuck her bottom lip out as if pouting, hoping to lend credibility to her comment.

Click, the line went dead. It seemed like forever before Miranda heard the familiar latch of the bathroom door, it slowly opened revealing Susan standing in the doorway, her bottom lip matched Miranda's. "How could I ever stay mad at you, baby thister." Susan mimicked what she sounded like when she said sister with missing front teeth.

"Aweeeee," Miranda said holding out her arms.

Susan threw her arms open and they embraced, each patting the other on the back. They giggled during the hug; Miranda realized they hadn't done that in some time, probably since Susan and Luke had begun going together. Miranda wanted to make the offer to drive her to the game, but she needed her cell phone first. That was the only way she could ensure Susan didn't warn her boyfriend she was coming. Then the idea struck her.

"Okay, change your shirt and I'll drive you to the game." Miranda said. "It's the least I can do. If Luke can't give you a ride home, I'll swing by and pick you up. That sound good?"

Susan said, "Okay, but I thought…" Miranda cut her off.

"Really, it's the least I can do, alright? Besides I know how you like to watch him play football, so c'mon, hurry, before I change my mind." Miranda said.

Susan grabbed her phone and checked it, no messages. She gave it a toss on her bed, and went into the bathroom to change.

Miranda waited until the moment the bathroom door closed, before she pounced on Susan's phone, quickly taking the back off of the flip phone, pulling the memory card out, rendering the ability to call or text completely useless. She put the cover back on seconds before the door opened again.

Whew, that was close. But she would have noticed the weight of the phone, had I taken out the battery. This way, she'll have no idea what's happened, until it's too late.

The two girls jumped in the car and headed to the school. Susan tried to send a text to her boyfriend, but the message failed. Miranda felt good, but at the same time she felt a little dishonest about the betrayal too.

Tales from the Silver State IV

"Can I use your phone to send a text to Luke? Mine is acting silly, I can't send a message." Susan said.

"Awe, mine's dead. I completely forgot to charge it before school this morning. We're almost there; will you be okay for a little bit?" Miranda asked.

"Yeah, I'll manage. I can use his phone if I need to." Susan replied.

They turned the corner on Fourth Street and saw the parking lot a block away. Miranda felt relief, this secrecy stuff was making her nervous, and she didn't like the fact that she had lied to her mother about needing the car, and disabled Susan's phone too. All of this caused Miranda's anxiety to go through the roof. But it would all be done and over shortly. She felt a smile creep across her face as she turned into the parking lot.

Miranda braked to a stop, more than half way from the field. "Okay," she said as the car came to a rest.

Susan looked at Miranda, "I thought you'd at least get me over to the gate, but I'll make this do," she said getting out of the car. "Thanks for the ride. I'm sure Luke'll bring me home after the game."

"Great, but if you need a ride, call." Miranda said, as she took off back through the parking lot. She turned on Fourth Street and drove out of sight. She waited a long and tenuous ten minutes, before turning around and driving back to the parking lot again. She stopped about half way and parked. Turning off the engine, she grabbed her phone and headed under the bleachers. She got as close to the field as she could and still be concealed from everyone's sight. Where she stood she could watch the field, and see anyone up on the bleachers, except for immediately above her.

Miranda scanned the field for lover boy, but didn't find him. She looked for Susan too, and not finding her, she went back to looking for Luke. Finally, she spotted him. Luke was with Martha Tate from the neighboring town, Boulder City, Nevada, located twenty miles away. Martha had developed late in life, but was making up for a tardy beginning by throwing herself at the boys. Whenever class was finished, you could find her wearing booty shorts, cut off so high up that her butt cheeks actually showed. That was bad enough, but she would cut the bottoms of her shirts off, and wear push-up bras, leaving the top buttons undone, in order to make the twins really noticeable. The boys were completely mesmerized by Martha's lack of restraint and flocked around her, whether attending a game, or the dance. The other girls despised Martha for her curves and late development.

From Miranda's viewpoint, it looked like Luke was pushed up against Martha, and his hand was on her butt, while his eyes fed on her chest. They were completely cozy, all smiles, flirting or whatever you call it.

Now Miranda needed to turn her attention to Susan. Where was Susan, and could she see what Luke and Martha were doing? She looked up to the top of the bleachers and all the way down to the football field, but didn't see her sister. At the risk of being spotted, Miranda stepped out from the bleachers and went to the gate so she could see who was directly above where she had been standing. Still no Susan.

As Miranda was thinking what she should do next, Susan walked out the side door of the school, just a few feet from the boy's locker room door, where, Luke had Martha.

"Oh My God", Miranda exclaimed. That's more than I had bargained for," she said. "Oh poor Susan,"

Miranda could hear shouting, and see Susan's arms swing around as she yelled at the pair. Luke had pulled away from Martha, and it was plain to see that they were afraid of Susan's anger. Susan swung hard at Luke. There was no mistake that Susan connected with Luke's face, Miranda could hear the crack and see the sting clear across the football field.

"Way to go Susan!" Miranda said. "Let that jackass feel it."

Miranda watched as Martha took off running from Susan, while Luke was rubbing his face, and walking away. When he pulled his hand away from his face, Miranda could see the bright red mark left by her sister. Susan now crumbled, falling to the ground and appeared to be in tears.

"Oh no, I better get over there and help her. She's not doing as well as I thought." Miranda said as she flew through the gate, running straight across the football field to her sister.

Tales from the Silver State IV

When she arrived Miranda dropped to her knees and said, "I'm sorry Suzzy. I'm so sorry that you had to see what Luke has been doing." Miranda said as she rapped her arms around her sister.

Miranda held her sister as she shook and cried, leaving Miranda wondering if she had done the right thing. Could she have done something differently? She doubted that. Now all she could do was comfort her sister, and hope for the best.

After what seemed like hours holding her sister, consoling her, whispering encouragement into her ear, Susan slowed to a whimper, her head jerking occasionally as she gulped for air. Finally, Susan stood up and embraced her sister. Miranda whispered into her ear, "Let's get out of here and go home. C'mon, I'll help you."

With their arms around one another, and Susan's head on Miranda's shoulder the two sisters walked back across the same field where Luke had been playing football earlier. Through the gate and out to the car. Miranda put her sister in the car first, then climbed into the driver's seat, started the engine, and drove home, while Susan stared out the window.

When they arrived home, Miranda went to the passenger side, retrieved Susan and helped her into the house. Mother saw Miranda helping Susan and came to see what had happened. Miranda briefly explained what occurred, but managed to leave out her part in the process.

Tales from the Silver State IV

They spent the next few hours consoling Susan, helping her return to reality. That night after Susan was in bed, Miranda had time to think about what had happened. She should have felt redeemed, that the whole thing was done and over with. But instead, she just felt terrible because she had facilitated this whole incident. Not facilitating Luke with Martha Tate, but arranged for Susan to witness Luke's infidelity. Miranda felt as though she had crushed her sister's spirit, her emotional stability was shattered after seeing what Luke was doing.

It was then that Miranda vowed to never tell Susan what she had done. Maybe once they had children of their own, she could mention it, but for now, it would remain Miranda's secret redemption.

BIRTH OF FREE AMERICA
By Edward Riepe

The time was seven P.M. when a black KIA and a Ford truck took a left off of Indios Avenue to head east on Boulder Highway. Cruising to the place on the highway to make a u turn to access the entrance to Trailrunner RV Park all eyes were on Row E.

"The two diesel pushers that were parked next to Karl's RV are gone. The big one with the four large slides is still there and so is the black SUV. What do you want me to do, Zak?" asked Ella.

"Cruise on in and stop for a second underneath the sign."

Ella did as ordered followed by Senior in his truck.

Once stopped, Tom eased out his passenger seat without saying a word and gently closed the door. Then he began to walk, not run, towards the remaining enemy RV.

"What is my husband doing?" asked Ella.

Tales from the Silver State IV

"Don't ask. Tom knows what he is doing. Move on to the showgirl's RV. I want you to get out and chat with them for a minute. Find out where Paulette is and tell them we have to get to the Strip because we have tickets. Don't forget to wish them Happy New Year. If they don't know where the girl is go across the aisle and knock hard on the door. If nothing happens…we have to go," said Zak.

"What about Tom?"

Zak paused for a brief moment before answering that question.

"Trust me. Tom will be back in that passenger seat before you return to the driver's seat."

Ella nodded her head but said no more. When she pulled up to the showgirl's RV they were sitting in two chairs enjoying the cool air and using their outdoor grill. Tied off to the leg of Sandy's chair was Paulette's mutt.

Ella exited the KIA and strolled up to talk with the women. Her chat with the two girls lasted three minutes, maybe a little longer. When she sat down in the driver's seat she was surprised to find Tom waiting.

He wasn't even breathing hard.

"Carol said that Rex and his brother came by with Paulette to ask if they would watch the dog while they went to the Strip. She said they had tickets to the top of the Stratosphere."

"I figured that might happen," muttered Zak.

"Where to now?" asked Ella.

"Head down Boulder to Sahara and when you get there hang a left," said Zak.

Ella looked at Tom and he had a cold stare on his face looking through windshield. It seemed to her that he was avoiding her look.

"That was quick. No one home I take it," she said as she put the KIA into gear.

Tom answered while staring ahead.

"One down…eighteen more to go," he said softly.

"What did you find inside?" asked Zak.

"That RV is basically a field hospital on wheels. That is where they used the heavy duty plastic wrap to seal off the back half of the vehicle. That is where they infected the four victims. The hallway closet if full of hazmat suits and medical stuff. The old man would have a field day in a coach like that," replied Tom.

"What did you do with the body?" asked Zak.

Tales from the Silver State IV

"I found him sitting on the shitter. That is where he remains."

"How?" continued Zak.

"Do I have to give you the details? There is no mess. That is an expensive vehicle."

* * * * *

Traffic was heavy heading west on Sahara Boulevard as was expected for this special night. During the trip there was little talk in the KIA. The atmosphere in the Ford truck was far different.

"I have been watching my rear view mirror since we left Trailrunner to check on your father and at every stop I have noticed that him and Karl seem to be hitting it off well," muttered Ella.

"I imagine so. Karl would chat with a brick wall if he thought it would talk back. Pop is the same way. Take a left here. Go down this side street a hundred feet or so and take a right into that empty field. That is where they kept the material when they were ...wait! What do you guys see ahead on the left side of the street? Is that our boys?" asked Zak.

Less than one hundred feet away were the two missing diesel pushers parked on the street headed north.

Tales from the Silver State IV

"Go past them to Riviera Street and make a u turn. If you can't find a place to park just stop on the street a good one hundred feet behind them and wait," ordered Zak.

"Wait for what? Granted, there isn't any traffic on this street but we can't be blocking the road!" exclaimed Ella.

"Will you quit questioning every order I give you? Doing shit like that could get someone killed tonight," hissed Zak.

"Lighten up, Zak. This is her real first ride. Do as he says, baby. If he tells you something that is fucked up I will step in and stop it. He usually does a damn good job," said Tom.

"Yes, sir," hissed Ella.

When the woman arrived at the t bone intersection with Riviera Street she yanked hard left on the steering wheel and punched the accelerator hard, spinning the rear wheels, causing them to smoke briefly. The KIA slid around one hundred and eighty degrees. As she passed by Senior and Karl in the old truck with eyes opened wide she performed her classic wave with her fingers while her passengers inside the KIA sat silently.

She glanced at Tom to see that now… he had a smile on his face and was shaking his head back and forth saying nothing. Zak, on the other hand, did say something, even if it was just one word.

Tales from the Silver State IV

"Women," he hissed.

Ella slowed to a stop one hundred and fifty away from the target RVs and watched in her rear view mirror as Senior executed a conventional three point turn with his truck. Then she heard the passenger door close once again and turned to see that Tom was, once again, gone.

"May I ask what Tom is up to?" said Ella.

"He is making space for us to park by the curb," replied Zak quietly.

Ella was looking ahead but could see nothing in the dark other than the cars in her headlights. Suddenly one car bolted from where it was parked, did a spin move similar to the one she had just performed and thrust over the curb, across the sidewalk to stop in someone's front yard.

"Wait for a second. He has to make room for Pop," said Zak.

Fifteen seconds passed when a second vehicle came to life. This time it was a Dodge truck and it was moving much slower. When the Dodge passed by she could see Tom at the wheel. She watched in her rear view mirror as the vehicle slowed and a figure clad in black from head to toe jumped out of the driver's door to let the vehicle continue on its path down the residential street to Riviera Street.

Tales from the Silver State IV

"Cops won't be coming to investigate that accident, not anytime soon, not on this night. Go ahead and pull in, driver. Everyone wait right here. He isn't done yet," said Zak calmly.

Ella parked and Senior pulled in right behind her. She killed her lights and turned off the motor. Then she saw Tom once again walking on the sidewalk passing by the passenger door this time in the direction of the large RVs parked by the curb.

Zak turned around in his seat and used a small flashlight to signal Karl sitting in the truck behind the KIA. Within ten seconds Karl was now sitting in Tom's seat. Without turning to face Lance, Zak or Little John sitting behind him he spoke.

"I have to take Fido for a walk."

"Ha! You owe me twenty bucks, Little John. I bet you he was gonna' take the dog for a walk this time!" exclaimed Lance.

Lance was already prepared. He had a rolled up wire in his left hand that glowed green in the dark. In his right he had a black leather beret. Karl took the two items, placed the beret on his bald head and stepped out of the KIA. Ella watched as he began to work with the wire, keeping it just below the line of sight of the passenger door. He then signaled Ella with his right hand.

Tales from the Silver State IV

"What?" asked Ella.

"He wants you to turn on the headlights for a brief moment. He needs some light. Turn them on for just a few seconds and then turn them off," ordered Zak.

Ella did as ordered. She watched as Karl bent over the right headlight, moving his arms back and forth. All the while he was looking at Ella with a smile on his face. She counted to five in her mind and turned the headlights off.

"Was that long enough?" she asked to no one in particular.

"It was," answered Zak.

She watched as Karl crossed the street to the sidewalk that ran beside the Fontainebleau security entrance.

"What in the hell?" she said.

"Karl is taking his invisible dog for a walk. I reckon it has to go shit…again," said Lance.

Extended in front of Karl was a glowing green wire that resembled a dog leash. At first glance, it looked like a man out taking his dog for a walk, only there was no dog at the end of the leash.

"Just watch. Vegas is full of crazy people," said Zak.

Tales from the Silver State IV

"That security entrance is too far away to see anything," said Ella.

Zak reached over the rear of the back seat, rummaged around for a moment to retrieve what he was after. He handed a pair of binoculars to Ella.

"Here. I want you to watch the Karl Show. The performances are rare and they are deadly. He is as efficient as Tom but doesn't have that agility because of his age but he is worth his weight in gold. Just watch."

Ella lifted the binoculars to scope out the terrain and Karl.

"He does look like he is walking an invisible dog. The guard ahead is dressed very familiar. Karl doesn't have his hand in his jacket pocket and I don't see any weapon," said Ella.

"The man is into knives, much like your bonded mate," said Zak softly.

The passenger door opened and Tom sat down.

"Two more down…sixteen to go," he said softly.

Ella lowered her binoculars to turn her head.

"You are going to miss the best free show in Las Vegas," said Zak.

Tales from the Silver State IV

Ella moved the binoculars back to her eyes and heard her husband's voice.

"Oh, yes. The Karl Show featuring the invisible dog...I wish we were closer. That works well when there is only a single guard."

There was a high, well built fence surrounding the field where materials were delivered years ago. Now the field was an empty vast area composed of gravel, populated by a small lighted guard shack at the entrance. The shack was designed for one man. The opening into the large field on the north side of the unfinished tower was eight feet in width. Karl brazenly turned left into entrance with his invisible dog and the guard, standing in front of his shack, moved quickly to intercept.

All Ella saw was the guard place his hand on Karl's right shoulder to spin him around. He succeeded. She watched as the glowing leash still in hand snapped to Karl's right, in a clockwise fashion, along with a subtle move of Karl's right arm.

Then the guard fell to the ground.

Karl grabbed the guard by his collar and opened the door to the guard shack. Briefly, Ella could see another man collapsed on the floor until Karl threw the enemy guard on top of him.

Then he slowly closed the door, turned and made a victory signal.

"How many fingers is he holding up?" asked Zak.

"Two," said Ella softly.

"One more down, fifteen to go," said Tom.

"Your math is off," said Ella.

"No it's not. One of Karl's fingers represented some poor dude who was making fifteen bucks an hour for pulling an easy assignment. That security guard is dead on the floor. It is time for us to go. It will take us a good hour, maybe longer, to get to the top of the Fontainebleau. That is one big ass resort," said Zak.

Everyone exited the KIA including Ella.

"Whoa… big girl! Where do you think you're going?" asked Zak.

"With you guys," replied Ella.

"No you're not. You stay here and guard our rides so we can get the hell out of Dodge if we get through this," ordered Zak.

"That's bullshit," hissed Ella.

Tom stepped in.

Tales from the Silver State IV

"Do what you're told. It's important and stay alert."

"Yeah? Sit on my ass in the KIA and stay alert for what?"

There was a pause in the conversation while Little John and Lance labored to remove the weapons from the rear. Finally, Zak turned to face Ella.

"Stay alert for any crazy fuckers out walking their invisible dog."

* * * * *

The four men headed for the security gate.

"Do you think she is pissed off?" asked Zak while walking.

"I think if we get by this night and get back to Ely I will be sleeping on the couch for a week or two, thanks to you," replied Tom.

"That is, if you get back. If things go south at least the kids will have someone to raise them."

"I reckon so. I see Karl rummaging around in the office trailer," said Zak.

"I would guess another man down, maybe two. Wanna' bet?" asked Tom.

"No."

Tales from the Silver State IV

The men climbed the four temporary steps and entered the office. On the floor were two men not moving, one dressed in black and the other wearing a security guard uniform.

"Fourteen to go. The odds are getting better," said Tom.

"The dead rag head or whoever he is saw me walking my dog and rushed outside to ask me what the hell was I doing. He is a big boy, a lot heavier than the one at the gate. I dragged him inside and the real guard was on the floor with his throat slit," said Karl nonchalantly.

"Let's get moving. We have a long ways to go and seventy floors to climb," said Zak.

"Wait! Actually it is only sixty eight floors to climb. I was looking at that large framed map hanging on the wall beside the door looking for any elevator locations," said Karl.

"Good idea but let's get busy. We don't have that long until midnight," added Zak.

"Uh oh. We are about to have company," said Lance while peering out of the entrance door.

Zak and Karl drew their Colts and had them in hand.

"Not that kind of company…well, maybe that kind of company for one of us," added Lance.

Tales from the Silver State IV

Strolling through the entrance doorway was Senior.

"Pop, I told you to stay with the getaway vehicles!" exclaimed Zak.

"Junior…you didn't tell me shit. You told Ella but…"

"Okay, Pop. So I didn't tell you but I did tell Ella so I thought you would speak with her."

"I did speak with Ella and I told her to come along but she said she had better stay and do what you told her to do. I could see steam coming out of her ears. Hell…she is in better physical shape then some of you boys. And I would like to add…Tommy… you probably won't be getting any pussy for a week or two if you survive this thanks to my son."

"I just assumed you would stay with the girl to watch out for her while we do our thing tonight."

"Junior, she ain't a girl anymore," said Senior.

"Then what is she?" asked Zak indignantly.

"She is a mom, an angry mom."

The freshly clean shaven Senior looked at his son and flashed a stern look.

Tales from the Silver State IV

"What are you boys doing? Having a water break? Having a smoke break?" asked Senior.

"We are looking at a wall map of the layout of the resort to find out where any elevators are located…that is if any are in operation," replied Karl.

"Of course there is an operational elevator, maybe more than one. Don't you see that fat ass security guard bleeding out on the floor? He hasn't climbed up a flight of stairs in years."

The five freedom fighters turned to look at the dead man on the floor while Senior headed for the door.

"Where are you going now?" asked Zak.

"Are you going to help Ella?" asked Karl.

Tom had been silently watching the family drama with a slight smile on his face. He had witnessed this play several times when he was young.

"I am headed out to the elevator. Tommy, you need to go ahead of me to clear out any problems. I will tell you where to go."

Tom moved to stand beside Senior…waiting.

"How do you know where to go? You haven't even glanced at the map," said Karl.

Tales from the Silver State IV

Senior framed a cold stare at Karl.

"Just go walk your dog."

"Please…how do you know?" asked Karl.

The old man relented to a degree. The ride with Karl from Ely had softened him but just a bit.

"Look outside. It is night. Just follow the lights," replied Senior.

Then he walked out into the field with Tom right beside him.

The remaining members of Free America turned to look at Junior.

"He is right. I hate it when he is right. Let's get moving."

* * * * *

The five men moved across the large empty field in the dark towards a cavernous building that had a large opening and lights, plenty of lights. Once there, Senior spoke.

"That is where we need to go. That is the receiving docks that were built for the big trucks. It reminds me of the receiving docks I saw one time at the Palazzo," said Senior.

"When were you in Vegas? You never told me," said Zak.

Tales from the Silver State IV

"When the Palazzo was completed I stayed there for a weekend to attend a doctor's convention at the Sands Exhibition Center. Walking from the Palazzo to the Sands you could see right into where the trucks were parked being unloaded. It was a busy place. Somewhere off that big room will be a hallway that will lead to the service elevators. They will be easy to find. Just follow the lights. The only question is will the bad guys have a guard posted in the hallway or at the elevator doors," stated Senior.

"Elevators? There is more than one?" asked Karl.

"Hell…yeah. Some are normal sized and some are big. Those are the freight elevators but they won't be on. This place is on a maintenance schedule and they are watching their expenses. There will be one that is in service. It probably only goes halfway up this large building. From there we follow the lights again to find the elevators that go to the top," concluded Senior.

"That sounds good to me, Pop. Tommy, you take the lead and everyone walk softly and move quietly," said Zak.

Ten minutes later the men were standing in a large elevator lobby. There were many doors but only one had a light displayed, just like Senior said.

"There is our ride. Tom, you know what to do. The fire stairwell is down at the end of this hallway," said Senior.

Tales from the Silver State IV

"I will send it back down in five or six minutes," said Tom.

He pushed the lighted button on the panel and the door opened. Inside, the men watched as he surveyed the floor display and pushed another button. The door closed.

"Why didn't we all get in?" asked Little John.

"We might be riding into an ambush doing that," said Senior.

"So you send Tom into harm's way?" asked Karl.

Senior looked at Karl and shook his head.

"I would never do that, at least intentionally. Tom is not stupid. If that elevator goes up to floor thirty six he will get off at floor thirty five and send it back down. If a guard is posted he will see that tattletale display counting as the elevator rises and suddenly goes back down. Tom will scoot up that stairwell to floor thirty six and make his move while that dummy is watching that display attempting to figure out what the hell is going on," said Senior.

Karl said nothing but nodded his head yes.

Three minutes later the door of the elevator opened. The five men walked inside.

Tales from the Silver State IV

"So we do the same thing?" Karl asked while moving to stand at the panel.

"You're learning," answered the old man.

"It does go up to the thirty sixth floor! How did you know that?" asked Karl.

"Lucky guess I reckon," answered Senior softly.

Once at the thirty fifth floor the men moved out into the hallway and headed south to the location of the stairwell. After climbing the stairs Karl found he was breathing hard. He wasn't sure if it was from the climb or the excitement. This was far more stressful than blowing up some IRS office in New Mexico with his Apache friends. He looked to see that Lance and Little John were also breathing hard. The only two members of Free America who seemed unfazed were Senior and Junior.

Zak looked the small doorway window to view the hallway.

"Tom is waiting," he said as he opened the door.

Karl looked over Zak's shoulder to see Tom halfway down the long hallway leaning against the wall. He was smoking a thin cigar. On the floor in front the elevator door was another body. Upon arrival to where Tom was waiting the five men saw that this time there was not a massive amount of blood from a knife wound. There was, however, a good sized hole in the guard's forehead that was trickling a small amount of blood.

"I didn't hear a shot," said Karl.

"Good," answered Tom.

He then held up his Colt with his right hand that was equipped with a long, custom made silencer.

"Where to now, old man? We still follow the lights?" asked Tom.

"Yep," answered Senior.

"Thirteen to go,' said Karl softly.

Tom locked eyes with Karl and slowly nodded his head yes. Then he fell in behind Senior while the others followed.

Tales from the Silver State IV

LONG TIME GONE
By Susanne Rowe

Get the hell out of here! He yells at the kids from the front porch and shuffles down the steps waving the shotgun. They ignore him until he shoots several rounds over their heads. That gets their attention and they race their dirt bikes up the mountain. The low light slants through the trees as darkness falls quickly over the tiny hamlet nestled at the base of the Spring Mountains. The wind started early that afternoon and seemed to herald the arrival of evil beings— he could hear the crashing of thunder in the distance and see lightning striking the peaks. The rain would begin soon and turn to snow when the temperature dropped with the setting sun. The roads would ice up too. He'd bring more wood inside the cabin so he wouldn't have to go outside during the storm.

Tonight is not a night for reading. The cold air whistles through the cracks in the walls and it bothers his arthritic hands. The man crawls under his heavy quilt and blows out the olive oil lamp he keeps on the stool beside the bed. The old dog shuffles over to its bed in the corner and turns several times moaning. *Shut up you,* the man mumbles. With a final groan, the dog settles down.

Tales from the Silver State IV

The man wakes just once in the night. He can hear the wind's eerie howling and maybe something else. Maybe coyotes? He reaches up from his bed and pushes the drape aside. He can see the snow is falling. He doesn't get up to look out into the yard but he knows the ground will be covered. The forecast called for cold weather the next three days, but at least the storm is supposed to break.

Early the next morning he wakes and painfully adjusts his hips so he can swing his legs off the bed. Rising, he shuffles to the kitchen, stirs the embers and adds more wood to the stove. He puts ground coffee and water in the blue enameled pot and sets it on top of the stove to brew. He pulls open the yellowed frilly curtains and notices a set of footprints crossing the yard. Puzzled he scans the frozen yard for other signs of a visitor. *One of those damn kids must have taken shelter on the porch last night and left after the snow stopped.* Judging by the amount of snow, the storm must have continued through the night. His coffee has finished brewing and he pours the steamy liquid into his ceramic mug. His fingers trace the chip in the handle. He watched the woman pinch the white clay and form the mug on her potter's wheel. How long has she been gone? Long time. The old dog still sleeps in its bed, twitching and sighing gently. The bare patches along its spine are spreading. He'll put the dog down this spring, before the heat of summer.

The man stands in front of the window watching the sun rise and the shadows under the trees dissolve. He notices the footprints lead across the yard to the cluster of trees where a small rise marks the edge of his property. The dirt road passes below. The footprints are clear in the crisp light. He can see their sharp edges in the fresh powdery snow. He finishes the coffee, sighs, and reaches for his parka hanging from the wooden peg. He struggles into its heavy bulk and pulls a wool cap over his bald head. The woman knitted the cap for him as a Christmas present. Or was it his birthday? So many years ago. Long time.

He takes his snow boots from the narrow closet next to the front door. Each boot holds a rolled woolen sock. What a ridiculous purple color. The neighbor down the hill near the highway knitted socks last year to sell as Christmas presents. She sold them out of her truck parked near the prison. No one bought the purple pair so she gave him the socks. He remembers hearing about some brother-sister act on the Strip. Didn't the brother always wear purple socks? He doesn't care, the socks are warm and he didn't pay for them. He sits on the small bench he cobbled together from cinder blocks and a salvaged plank. He pulls on the socks, groaning with the effort. He hurts more this morning from bending over yesterday as he gathered broken branches for kindling and hauled extra firewood inside.

The man laces his boots, then unlatches and unlocks the cabin's front door and steps out onto the porch. He quickly closes the door behind him keeping the heat in the tiny cabin. The air is icy. He takes a shallow breath and feels the pain in his lungs. He exhales and his breath fogs. He takes thick wool mittens from the pocket of the coat and struggles to pull them over his gnarled fingers. Even through the mittens he can still feel the frozen cold of the stair rail. He takes his time stepping down the three steps, holding the rail tightly. A fall this far from town could be fatal. He would lie there and freeze to death. He shakes his head banishing the thought. He reaches the bottom step and the concrete landing. It is covered with a foot or more of fluffy white powder. His boots sink until the snow reaches the boot tops where the thick purple socks peek out. He carefully steps beside, but stays clear of the footprints. He might decide to call the sheriff to report the trespasser.

He crosses the yard slowly. It is bright, so bright. His eyes hurt and he squints. The sun reflects a thousand thousand—a million and more—sparkles like the dancing fireflies he remembers from his trip to Missouri to meet his in-laws years ago. The landscape there was moist and green. The woman had loved the flowers in her parents' garden. They had picked vegetables from that garden and thrown them on the grill. He ate the meat and potatoes. He still didn't like vegetables, even grilled.

The woman had loved the tiny cabin. They'd been happy there or so he thought. He'd only slapped her the one time. He didn't even remember how it had happened exactly. It was hot and she'd let the dog in after swimming in the creek. There was a foul stench hovering over the dog as if he'd rolled in a dead animal. He'd yelled at her to keep the dog out—he'd been cleaning his gun, but in they came. The dog had jumped up on the couch and knocked his coffee over. Maybe that was when the handle had chipped. Long time ago.

To make it up to her, to ask forgiveness for the slap, he had dug up and replanted a couple of western redbuds they'd seen growing in the foothills. Although the elevation at the cabin was a bit high for redbud, one of the saplings had thrived in the front yard sheltered from the icy winds coming off the mountain. She loved that little tree. Now its full branches spread across the yard. In the spring it was a mass of blooms even before the soft heart-shaped leaves could break. He had seen tourists from town pull off the road and take photos of the redbud with their cell phones.

Many evenings he would sit on his porch in the dusk and watch the youngsters on their motorbikes racing up the road. He knew they were headed to the old Boy Scout campground. He saw them speed past and heard them yelling, planning to party up in the abandoned campground although this week he knew the conservation crew would have warned them about the approaching storm. He'd seen the work crew pack up their gear and drive out early that afternoon. They weren't fools. The wind was bad here at Sliver Creek and gusts had been clocked at ninety miles an hour. He supposed the kids thought they'd stay warm snuggled up with Jim Beam or Jose Cuervo. He remembers the one night that hadn't happened. They'd staggered down the road at midnight hooting and hollering. His was the first cabin they'd reached and they'd pounded on the door. He'd answered them all right—waving his shotgun and firing over their heads. Now they left him alone.

The back of the old man's cabin faced Bonanza Peak. Bonanza wasn't a destination like Mount Charleston. In the Spring Mountains, Charleston received all the attention as the highest peak. No, there weren't many hikers or campers coming up Camp Bonanza Road to climb Bonanza Peak. He recognized most of the kids and their friends from the village. But one fine spring day he'd seen a beautiful young girl and her young man walking up the road. He watched them from the shadows of the pine trees at his property line. They were wearing backpacks and sturdy leather boots. He'd watch out for those two.

The young girl looks at the tiny cabin and sighs wistfully. She is newly pregnant and she and her young husband do not want to raise their future family in Las Vegas. Although Sliver Creek is a bit remote, there is a bus that takes the children to nearby Indian Springs for school. She had talked to the locals. She is fair skinned and ethereal with clouds of soft red hair. Her husband is short and solid. He put himself through college working construction so he is not only educated but handy. He has wanted to live off the grid for years.

Tales from the Silver State IV

Several days later the old man sees the couple walking down the mountain past his cabin.

The young woman calls the realtor to ask about the little cabin up the hill. As it turned out, the young woman had gone to school with his son. Now she's married and pregnant and they don't want to live in the city. The realtor lives in the mountains too, but farther south in Kyle Canyon. Although he owned land in Sliver Creek, the realtor isn't fond of the community. He thinks living off grid brings out the survivalists and misanthropes. He wasn't crazy about the government and he hated the local politicians, but he isn't an anarchist either. *Go along to get along,* that was his motto. At least Sliver Creek had a community well. Monthly homeowners' dues paid for piped filtered water and a snow plow to clear the roads in winter. Those who bought property inside the homeowners' association tended to be more compliant than those living outside the community in their trailers and shipping containers. Those folks either dug their own wells or had water delivered from town. There was even one old guy rumored to carry water up from the creek. That was frightening. The realtor had seen a mustang die in that creek. The coyotes had eviscerated the animal and all those body fluids had floated downstream. He flinches at the thought.

The young woman chats with the realtor. "What a cute little cabin! Too bad it's been neglected."

Tales from the Silver State IV

"It's been vacant for some time now. The old man who lived there was a recluse. He was always threatening the local kids. The sheriff thinks maybe the old guy heard a noise one night during a bad storm. They found tracks leading from his house to those pine trees next to the road. The coroner said he had a heart attack and fell hitting his head against a rock. He was frozen solid when the neighbors could finally get out and check on him. It should have been sad; however, he was a mean old cuss. The kids say that cabin is haunted. Are you sure you're interested?"

"Oh that doesn't bother us. I like to think the old guy would appreciate us living there and watch out for us. We'll fix it up real nice."

Night falls and the old man goes to bed. As he crawls under the thick starburst-patterned quilt he thinks about his grandma. Now there was a real woman, he knows he comes from good stock. Not like that young one that's stealing his cabin or so she thinks. But he'll deal with her. He notices the dog is gone. Long time gone. It must have wandered off or maybe the coyotes killed it. He hasn't seen it and that's good. It saves him the cost of a bullet.

RETURNING HOME

By Thom Slaughter

I stand here frozen in fear. I cannot remember a time in my life when I have felt more afraid. My hands are shaking and my mouth is dry. Shifting my weight from leg to leg is the only way I have kept my knees from buckling. As I stand here, I think back to the events that have brought me to this point in my life.

I grew up not far from this spot. Our apartment was on the outskirts of Las Vegas. The place was rundown even when it was new. My Mother had to work two jobs to feed, clothe and ensure there was roof over the head of my brother and three sisters. I was the oldest, but there were not that many years separating any of us. I grew up not knowing my Father and my Mother never spoke of him. I can remember only small flashes of him. I remember the fighting and the yelling. The police came one night and I have not seen him since. There wasn't much to do for kids in Vegas, so I found myself in a gang at an early age. They were my family. I learned about the streets from them, how to survive. My gang family taught me how to steal things that I wanted…that my Mother could not afford. I was good at lifting items from stores, the trick was to buy something small and take something expensive. My Mother caught me once when I gave some earrings I had swiped to my sisters. She took a wooden spoon to my backside. I don't think I sat down for a week. I told my gang family what had happened and they laughed and laughed…they said it was part of the life.

Once I got caught by a store manager and he called my Mother. She had to leave work to come and get me or the man said he was going to turn me over to the police. After the spoon, my Mother marched me down to the church to talk with our priest, He nearly bored me to death with all of his preaching about "Thou shalt not steal" and where I would spend eternity if I did not change my ways. That did not stop me from stealing. Then my gang taught me about tagging. They showed me how to spray our gang symbol. I began to tag walls…small and hidden at first. The other members in the gang thought I was good, so my tags got larger and more colorful. I began to be known for my tags. I had developed my own style…my own signature. Other gangs started to notice as well. My tags began to become defaced…my gang family said that they had disrespected us and that we should take care of them. I had never thought of my tag as being permanent. I knew the city would come and clean it off or paint over it, so it did not bother me that someone else covered it up. I made excuses that my Mother made me stay home. I knew I would have to face being teased, but I wanted no part in violence. Maybe my Mother had passed something on to me after all. Or maybe it was something I had seen when I was young.

I did like art classes at school. The teacher showed me how to make things look more realistic with shade and shadow. I began to try everything I learned in art class in my tags. Sometimes it worked sometimes it didn't. When it didn't my gang family let me know. They were my harshest critics. After a few failures I stopped trying new things in my tags. I stayed doing what I knew. I barely saw my brother and sisters anymore. My brother had gotten into drugs and one of my sisters had run away from home. My Mother looked older and more tired every time I saw her. I did not know how to talk to her so I didn't. I spent more and more time away from home. When I was not at home I was out in the desert. The desert was a good place to get away. At times I would take what I saw out there and try and draw it from my memory in art class. I did not always get that right either, but my art teacher did not laugh, she took the time to admire and show me how to make things better.

My sister that had run away returned home one day... she had gotten pregnant. She was only thirteen and she said that the man that she had been with was in his twenties and threw her out when he found out. That was the one time I felt violent. I wanted to take every bit of rage and take it out on his hide, but my sister would not tell us who he was. Mother was so concerned and brought her to see the priest. The police came to our house again and again to interview my sister, but she would not tell them who had gotten her pregnant. My sister wanted to keep the child, but my Mother convinced her to give it up for adoption. Mother asked what kind of life she thought she could give the child…she told her to look around… to look at me at our other brother. She cried for days, but finally she agreed. The Priest helped to set that up as well. After the child was born my sister seemed empty…she withdrew to her room and began to take drugs with my brother.

I saw what drugs did to my brother and sister and never wanted to take them. They said that it made them forget…that they could escape all this. I would give them money when I could spare it, but soon they were taking more and more. My other sister threw herself into school. She always came home and studied. One night a teacher came home with her. I thought she was in trouble, but the teacher was there to ask if she could take my sister on a trip to our capital…that she had won some sort of award. Mother said she couldn't go. I knew that my Mother wanted to let her go, but we could not afford it. My sister said that the trip was paid for, but my Mother would not take charity.

Tales from the Silver State IV

I decided I would make enough to send my sister. I stopped giving money to my other siblings for drugs, no matter how much they begged. A week before the trip I had made enough and gave an envelope to my sister, I told her to go and enjoy herself. Mother asked me where I had gotten the money… but I refused to answer. She told me I was still not too big for her to take a spoon to.

The day after my sister left for her trip, my brother overdosed on drugs. The paramedics tried their best to revive him but hey had arrived too late. Mother wanted to call my sister and tell her. I persuaded her not to say anything… he was not going to be any less dead and why ruin her trip. My brother's funeral was scheduled for after my sister's return.

The whole thing was sad, although I never shed a tear. I had lost my brother years ago when he had sold himself for the poison that consumed him. He was always chasing that first high…his body and who I knew as my brother withered away long ago. At the funeral I saw so many relatives I had never seen before. Many of my gang family came out as well. My Mother gave them dirty looks…she blamed them for my brother's death.

Mother was determined not to lose any more of her kids. The day after my brother's funeral, I came home to a priest, a social worker and a couple of Mother's friends and my other sisters. I stopped thinking that they were there for me, but Mother motioned me to sit down and handed me a script. I was to tell my sister what she meant to me and how much her drug use hurt me. Standing, I shook my head and dropped the sheet of paper on a chair and went to the kitchen I grabbed a drink and left by the kitchen door. I wanted my sister to get help, but I figured that drugs, probably had a stronger hold on her than these people could break. I went to meet my gang family under a bridge. I wanted to be anywhere but at my house. When I finally did go home I found out that my sister had agreed to go to some sort of drug rehabilitation program and my other sister had been accepted into some sort of educational program…that left one sister and myself at home with my Mother.

The next few months were hard…Mother was let go from one of her jobs. It was a lot harder to sneak out of the house. Every time I tried to go somewhere she insisted on knowing where and who I was going with. I finally was able to get out one night when she went to bed early. I had been working on a tag for a couple of days…it was going to be one of the largest pieces I had ever done. I was almost done when I saw the flashing lights come up behind me. Then the voice came over the loud speaker telling me not to move. I knew I had been caught. I was taken to jail. They called my Mother and she told them I could just stay there. I was transferred over to the juvenile facility. I sat there for several

Tales from the Silver State IV

days before I was scheduled to see a judge. When my day came I had expected to have a lawyer like you always see on television and in the movies, but when I arrived there was only a social worker there waiting for me. The woman told me there was someone else waiting to see me. I was expecting to see my Mother but when the courtroom door opened there stood my art teacher. She stood before the judge and defended my character. Afterwards I was released to the social worker. My art teacher was to be responsible for me during weekdays and she would file reports. My Mother reluctantly agreed to be responsible for me on the weekends. I now had a curfew, and I had to stay away from my gang family. I only had two years left in school and then I could be away from all of this. At first I hated everything. I went to school, did my work and that was all I did. My teacher encouraged me to carry around a journal to record my thoughts. Then she had me drawing in my journal. Each semester she reviewed my grades helping find me tutors. Every day she would spend time helping me with my drawings…she introduced me to an army vet at an afterschool program that painted desert landscapes. I learned everything he was willing to teach. My grades improved and during my senior year I had an art show at a local gallery, she even helped me to apply to colleges. I was so surprised when I was accepted. I did not know how I could possibly have gotten in until I found out that my teacher had submitted a portfolio of my art along with letters of support from her and others. I had a full scholarship and a job when I got there. I did not have to worry about anything, but having time to study.

Now I was back in Vegas. I was not far from my old apartment. This was no longer the edge of town. Many things had changed, but many things had not. There were many graffiti tags on walls around the neighborhood. I recognized the same sort of gang members that I grew up with. My fear was growing with every minute that passed. I stood here with my knees shaking…then the dreaded sound… the cacophony of noise that thundered into the room. I felt like throwing up. Then silence.

"Good morning…I am going to be your art teacher this year."

MOURNING SACRIFICE
By Tonya Todd

A bleached moon glowed behind black velvet clouds. The violet sky twinkled with possibility as I drove to Selene's apartment, same as I had for the last six months. Darkness fell early now, lengthening my time with her. The air smelled fresh though likely I imagined it in my anticipation of her company.

I drove past the spot where her husband died. There were faster routes, but each night I ventured by to remember. His disappearance caused this dream wrapped in nightmare. Without it, she'd not trouble with me. She'd have no need.

Finding his body, determining his fate—those were her only purpose. The Henderson police had failed her, and that's where I came in. Each night, assisting her search. Each night, her mournful eyes. Each night, my torment renewed.

She'd sent a text about a new lead. A safe house. Whatever it was, she'd not find him, but I would accompany her just the same. She had no one else after all.

Her door swung open as soon as I knocked. She greeted me with a smile, the way she had of late. The sadness remained, but less severe each evening. Sterling spirals, hanging from her lobes, matched those of her ebony curls. I allowed my gaze to linger as I too often did.

Blood rushed to her cheeks—subtle beneath her dark skin, but impossible for me to miss. Typically, her face held me captive, but tonight my eyes fell to her apple red dress. Latex by the scent.

"A costume, *cara*?" I forced my focus higher.

"In case we get caught."

"How will this help?"

She smirked. "The non-enlightened will assume I'm a hooker."

"A senseless assumption. Let us hope it does not come to that." I offered my elbow to her. "Ready?"

"Almost. Come inside while I finish."

"Inside?"

"Of course. I don't know why you still wait out there after all this time." She backed up to allow my entrance.

With caution, I crossed the barrier into her home. The room struck me with a rich Selene bouquet. I shut my eyes to calm my senses. She was everywhere.

"Will you zip me?" She turned and braced herself against the wall, her snug dress open to the small of her bare back. Was this a test?

My fingers trembled as I reached for the tab. "This gets tighter?" I inhaled, bathing in her fragrance, cinching the zipper's teeth slower than I should. Why did she tempt me so?

Tales from the Silver State IV

"Finito." I sucked in one last whiff.

She padded across beige carpet to a nearby closet. When she emerged, tall, spike-heeled boots gloved her luscious legs.

"Can you walk in those?" I asked, ashamed to enjoy the visual.

"Better than you'd think."

"I think you can do anything."

Again, she smiled my way, infecting me with undeserved joy. I should never have stepped inside.

I looked elsewhere while she applied her lipstick, a practice she'd resumed six weeks ago. Rows of photographs decorated her walls. One in particular caught my eye— Selene, infant in hand, husband by her side.

I admired the blended palate of the trio. A mating of one so fair with one dark as Selene would have been shunned during my last visit to the Americas. Much like my kind where some are born and others made, intermixing was discouraged.

The tiny child appeared helpless in her arms, a half-breed, much like myself. "Only six days, you said?"

She sighed, her gloom returning. "Maybe they're together now."

Why had I brought it up? I touched her shoulder to comfort.

She shivered.

"Shall we?" I hoped to escape the grim mood.

Tales from the Silver State IV

Nodding, she addressed her husband's picture. "Don't worry, baby. I'll find out what happened to you. Tonight. I know it." She kissed the glass, leaving a crimson print, and then stroked the frame. Her farewell revealed the absence of jewelry on her left hand.

"Where is your—"

She twirled to face me, and I swallowed the vision, every captured curve committed to memory.

"How do I look?"

Quelling my first response—inspired—I settled for, "A coat, I think."

She fetched a long trench from her closet and returned to take my arm. "Let's go."

Selene's neighbor gasped when we stepped out. She hobbled by, hissing as we passed. Her tendency to clutch her cross and chant when I came round didn't faze Selene who spoke not a lick of Italian. The warnings fell on her lovely American ears, creating no disharmony.

My accidental glance left the woman slack-jawed and frozen. I tipped my fedora, a habit I hadn't outgrown from an older time—not my own, but old nonetheless—and smiled at her. She scurried into her home and slammed the door.

"Well, that was rude," Selene said once in the car.

"Perhaps, she worries about…" I turned away. "A *man* in the house."

"It's really none of her business."

Tales from the Silver State IV

"She means well, *cara*."

Selene dropped the topic to direct me toward the first stop, a bar in downtown Las Vegas. She peered my way when we stopped at a light. "Why were you named D'artagnon?"

My name called me back to the night she'd first asked for it. After another fruitless search, I'd feared she meant to check my credentials, a task she'd neglected in the burden of her grief. Fool that I am, I'd answered in truth.

"Like the musketeer?" she'd asked.

"Something like that. Call me Dan."

"No," she'd insisted. "It's not your name."

She was divinity itself.

Honking cars propelled me to the present. The light was green. "Why do you ask?"

"Isn't it a last name? His first name was Charles."

"Did your research, *cara*?" When she didn't respond I explained. "My mother was a fan." His mistress, in fact.

"Are you French or Italian?"

"Who's the detective here? You're full of inquiries tonight."

She flipped her hair aside, tossing her scent my way.

"You know all about me, but I never asked your story. You've been so dedicated, so helpful." She touched my wrist. "I need to thank you somehow."

"This job." The heat from her fingers branded my arm. "Reward enough."

Tales from the Silver State IV

"There must be something I can do for you." Her lashes blinked with a heavy clap. Her heartbeat filled the front seat.

I loosened my collar, then lowered the windows to let in the city—the buzz of neon, whirring tires, anything but the enticement within reach.

Her mahogany skin paled. I realized in horror that in my distraction, I'd driven past the Smith Center. Where I'd discovered her.

In my obsession of the latest Sibella, I'd followed the production of "A Gentleman's Guide" to Las Vegas. On the final evening performance, *she* entered my sight. *Selene.* Silver sparkles from her gown rippling over her curves as she descended the grand staircase.

She reminded of my first love, before the change, though she bore no resemblance to Aeliana. Different in every way save for the grace in her step and the sway of her rounded hips. Never in my boundless years had I been struck with such devastation as to spot Selene, love her in an instant, then watch her ardent gaze adore another.

Spite overtook me. I followed them home where the cries of coital bliss pierced their closed window. Consumed with lust and envy, I trailed him to a nearby corner mart when he left to fetch more wine. Every ounce of my blood seethed.

I robbed her of her husband that night. Drained him of every precious drop. Centuries of coveting the living, suffering my admiration from a distance, longing for the mortal life I'd never reclaim, all culminated in one fatal moment.

I simply snapped.

And now I serve my penance: aiding her search, watching her grieve, witness to her sorrow. But, never allowing my advance.

My moment of weakness destroyed the life she'd made. To compensate I'd ease her woes and protect her from the monsters in the world. "My apologies, *cara*. I meant to avoid this."

"It's fine." She sank into the seat. "Do you think I'll ever find him?"

She wouldn't, though I knew not what to say. Ending the chase might bring closure. Yet, if her quest gave her purpose, I'd not steal that from her, too.

"Tell me I'm not kidding myself."

I parked the car, then turned to search her forlorn eyes. I could take her grief from her, relieve her of those memories, but that seemed a worse theft than that of her husband. "What I think matters not."

Her eyes darted down when I helped her from the passenger side. "It does to me." Her fingers slipped through mine. "The cops think he left me." Without his body or car as evidence, they'd dismissed the case. "We were finally healing. Finally happy again. Even trying…" She clutched her abdomen.

Tales from the Silver State IV

"No tears tonight." I thumbed her cheek though none had fallen. "They'll not help your search."

She lurched forward and embraced me. Another breach in my resolved constraints, yet my witless arms obeyed. Holding her close, I basked in her warmth. All of me hungered for her.

"You always make me better." Her heart rate slowed and she smiled up at me.

Seized by her beauty, my fool mouth spoke. "He would never leave you, Selene. No man could."

"How do you know?"

"The way he looked at you." I released her and turned my head. "In the photographs."

She accepted my lie, and we accessed the bar. The dead room housed only a few scattered couples and a small group of university lads—footballers by their jerseys, and perhaps a ball boy.

Over the course of our investigation, I'd noted Selene's theatrical flair when occasion called for it. This night, as she crossed the room, her working girl swagger drew every eye. The resulting face slap from a jealous wife did not stop the ogling of one onlooker. He rubbed his cheek, then employed a more furtive glance.

Though I wished to crush his skull, I could not blame the man. Selene had entered without her coat, showcasing her perfection. I, too, struggled to veer away.

Tales from the Silver State IV

I held sentry at the door while she questioned the barista. From that distance I heard their exchange. He said little of value at first, but did claim to have directions to the safe house. When a customer interrupted, my discipline failed and I glimpsed Selene's way. She turned round and leaned back against the bar with her legs outstretched.

Had I a beating heart, she'd still it.

I followed the length of her lithe form from the vinyl boots, up her shiny dress, and settled at her plump, cherry lips. The night would be long indeed.

The pack of boys passed by to exit, breaking my line of vision. I caught a whiff of their youth and decided a top off might be in order to control myself with Selene. Flashing the shield that purports as my badge, I plucked away the weak one. "Detective Caccia. A word, if you please."

"A-am I in trouble?" His cherub cheeks rouged.

I zeroed in on his eyes. "Fear not, young one. Tell your friends you'll catch up, then meet me round back."

This age of voyeurs made reporters of anyone with a smartphone. With discretion in mind, I surveyed the lot. Nothing stirred.

The boy joined me as instructed. I swept the area again, then extended my canines. Even paralyzed under my thrall, his muscles tensed when I pricked his soft flesh.

So young.

So supple.

Tales from the Silver State IV

His smooth, tangy delight seeped into me, and in that sweet moment, I forgot her. Feeding was the only time I could. Once temporarily sated, I healed his wound and suggested we hadn't met.

He stumbled away as a familiar scent pulled me toward the bar's entrance. *Selene.* I checked for any spills and rushed to meet her. "Where to now?"

She slipped me the address on a torn sheet of paper. "Where'd you go?"

"To handle a leering boy." I dabbed my mouth again.

"It's sweet of you to protect me, but I don't care what they think. I just need answers." Her hand stroked my arm. "Otherwise, I'll never be able to…" She edged forward, eyes wide, but my renewed strength allowed me to back away. "What does it matter?" she snapped. "If he's dead, there's no one left to miss me."

"*Cara*, please."

"Be honest." She stepped closer. "If I quit searching, would you even bother with me? Would I see you again?"

I stared into her dark eyes, black as my tainted soul. "Every night. Until you tired of my company."

Her hot breath scathed my chin. "What are you saying?"

Again, I retreated. "Only that… I'll not desert you."

"That's all?"

"That's all." I turned my back to her and headed for the car.

Tales from the Silver State IV

Her information brought us to a government home near Balzar Avenue, a neighborhood typically buzzing with sin. The stillness of the street implied an unseen threat. I asked Selene to stay behind while I assessed the danger. Even a ruse could provide real peril.

Beer bottles and cigarette droppings ornamented the front stoop. I cased the perimeter, then listened inside. The only sound detected, light clacking approaching from behind: Selene, who never could obey. One more aspect to treasure.

"Recently abandoned," I said when she reached me.

"Let's try inside." She revealed a tiny, metal pick from a leather sleeve and crouched before the door.

I watched in awe while she worked the tool. The device scraped inside the lock until a distinct click gave way and the knob turned. "Where did you learn that?"

"I lived a very different life before." She waved me inside and I froze.

"Ladies first?" I offered at a loss.

"Oh," she said. "I thought you'd want to check it." She stared up at me with the expectant eyes of one in the presence of a hero.

As the villain who'd ruined her life, I forged my valor and attempted to cross the door's threshold. No force prevented my entry.

The stink of booze, smoke, and violence saturated the air. One superseding aroma beckoned me deeper within the dwelling. Fangs itching, I tracked the scent to the furthermost bedroom.

A man, beaten and bruised, hunched limply on a chair. Duct tape and rope prevented his collapse. His faint heart whispered its defeat, yet *his* blood had not summoned me.

Beneath a second chair, a dark pool congealed. A trail streaked the floor, thinning as it approached the attached bathroom. My senses informed me that no one remained, yet I checked inside to be certain. Empty, save for the red-stained blade.

"What happened here?" I asked.

The man shifted as though he'd just noticed my presence. His sallow eyes begged the removal of his gag. I loosened the cloth as Selene entered the room.

Her eyes popped. She covered her mouth as if stifling a scream that wouldn't erupt. The man tried to speak, but Selene's trembling distracted me from his words.

I ushered her toward the door. "Look away, *cara*. This is not for you."

"No." She shoved by me. "I need to see. I have to know. Was it...?"

The man's raspy plea killed the terrible silence. "Help," he whimpered. "They butchered him."

"Who?" Selene demanded. "Where is he?" She dashed to the chair and tugged at ropes that did not budge.

"Don't know his name," he grunted. "Need a doctor."

Tales from the Silver State IV

"We'll get one." She pulled uselessly at his bindings. "Is he alive? Where is he?"

"Dead. Saw where they're headed."

"Tell us!" She jerked the ropes in a frenzy.

"Let me, Selene." I examined the Gordian knot and determined Alexander's method best. "Fetch the knife." I pointed to the bathroom. "Use a towel to avoid prints."

"Isn't it evidence? Should you call this in?"

"Not if you want to get there first; now hurry." In her absence, I commanded the man's cooperation. When she returned, I cut him loose.

"Mountains." He spoke between wheezing. "Up west."

"Can you draw it?" I asked.

Selene scrambled for pen and paper. From the comfort of the floor, the man sketched a rough map of where they absconded with the body whose essence had guided my discovery.

One phony call to my fictitious precinct, and we rushed to the car. Though I knew the voyage to be a farce, Selene's adrenaline galvanized. Ignoring all traffic laws, we raced to Mt. Charleston to recover the corpse.

The moon lit our way toward a deserted lee off the mountainside. At that elevation the October winds chilled enough that Selene cinched her coat. Determined to find the body that was not her husband, she limped along the rocky path, jagged terrain quarreling with the tender feet within her merciless boots.

When her struggle became too much for me, I scooped her up to cradle her in my arms. She did not argue as expected, but instead settled against me, possibly hoping for warmth she'd not receive. All my worldly desires snuggled against my shoulder, trusting me with her life, yet I carried her toward a risk my actions created.

"These men are dangerous," I said. "We'll go if they're still here."

"No," she whispered. "Tonight's the night. I can feel it."

"I won't gamble your life."

"I have faith."

How she could hope after all she'd lost, I could not comprehend. But, by the grace of her credence, no living men remained near the site. Only ash and footprints marked the presence of the disposal crew.

They'd concealed the grave well from human eyes, beneath rock and bush. I spotted it straight away, yet allowed her search to validate the sham, then pretended to stumble upon it.

Substituting a flat rock for a spade, I uncovered the corpse. The anguish in her face when she realized we'd reached another dead end maimed me to my core.

Tales from the Silver State IV

"It's not him." Her eyes glistened. "I'm never going to find him. Never know what happened." She raced down the mountainside until a patch of soft dirt gripped her heels.

As a reflex, I pursued and caught her with ease. Squelching my hunter's urge, I reached out to soothe Selene who flew into my arms where she bawled with abandon. My heart broke for the pain I'd caused my beloved.

She deserved the truth.

Her shuddering stopped. "It's over." She looked up at me, her ardent gaze disarming my confession. "I'm done."

Paralyzed with desire, I stood, helpless, while she tested her lips on mine.

Her coat dropped.

My resolve crumbled.

I reached for her zipper while she tugged at my shirt and trousers. Her dress peeled away, and I pounced: kissing her, licking her, suckling at her breast.

My fangs emerged.

I froze.

"We can't." I turned from her. "Your husband."

"Don't you see? He's dead."

Again, I swallowed my urges.

"He's not coming back," she said. "There's no betrayal."

"There is." I willed my fangs away. "I'm not truly a detective."

Tales from the Silver State IV

"Then…" She covered her bare breasts. "What are you?"

My stomach seized. "A monster. Who wished to help."

"Well, you did." She sauntered closer, exposing herself to me. "You helped me track every lead. Helped me accept the truth." Her warm fingers reached into my hair. "Now help me heal."

One brush of her tongue on my neck and I faltered. "Please." My arms wrapped around her. "Stop."

"I need you," she begged. "Don't reject me."

"This isn't what you think." With effort, I restrained myself. "I'm not… human."

She cowered away snatching my shirt from the ground to cover herself. "Look, if you're not into this, just take me home."

"Selene."

She glared back.

"*Vieni qui, cara*. Come here."

She tiptoed forward.

"I won't harm you." My lips curled to show her.

She fingered my canines, then flinched. "H-How..?"

"Touch my skin. You had to notice."

She smoothed her hand over my cheek, down my neck, and across my chest. "Impossible."

"I'm sorry."

Her brow arched. "This is why. Only at night."

Tales from the Silver State IV

"*Sì.*"

She raised her brave chin and peered into my soul. "It changes nothing."

"It changes everything."

"No." She cast off the shirt, sanctioning the brisk night to stiffen her already pert nipples. "I want you." She swept her curls off her shoulder. "If you want me, I'm yours." Her pulse ignited. "Take me!"

I lunged for her and spoke against her throat. "You don't know what you say."

"I do."

"No, *cara.*"

"Without you this year, I'd have ended my life. You believed in me. Kept me sane." The heat from her bosom warmed my lifeless chest. "Help me move on." She returned to my lips: kissing me, scraping her tongue along the daggers in my mouth, pressing just enough to kindle the flame.

The trickle fevered my thirst. Drove me beyond rational thought.

Her throbbing jugular. Her svelte body. Their pleas for penetration.

I obliged them both.

I hurled her down on the coat, thrust deep within her, and pierced her willing flesh. Her initial cry rippled through me as the sweet copper flood gushed over my tongue. The orgy of thrills overwhelmed my senses—her screams of pain and pleasure, a symphony for my bliss. I lost myself in her, drowning in ecstasy, dreaming to make her mine. Truly mine. For eternity.

But, she was not mine.

"I can't." With all my strength, I stopped. My body tremored from the inertia. "C-Can't do this to you."

"I want you to," my temptress purred.

I closed my eyes to resist. "It was me." Fighting sobs, I opened them to prove my sincerity. "I killed him."

"You didn't." She shook her head. "You couldn't."

"I did."

She scrambled back and covered herself, crouching, crying, bleeding. "No."

"*Mi dispiace.*" I knelt before her. "I'm so sorry."

Her furious eyes narrowed. "How could you tell me? Why did I have to know?"

"My love forced my confession. I don't deserve you."

She snatched a rock, heaved it at me, and missed. "You... you monster."

"*Sì.*"

"*You...*" She grabbed a fallen branch and broke it in half. Wielding it as a stake, she came at me on her knees, lunging for my heart.

I accepted her attack, ineffective as it was. Merely a scratch.

"Stand up," she screamed, doing the same.

I obeyed.

Tales from the Silver State IV

She stabbed again, throwing her weight into it. The point cut deeper, yet not enough. She shrieked and flung the stick at me.

The bright moon highlighted a clearing. She hastened there and dislodged a stick from the ground. A narrow, wooden tent spike. Perfect for the task.

She charged at me, and I braced for her vengeance. The rod drove through, gouging me, yet failing once again. She'd not pushed deep enough, nor was her aim correct.

"I hate you." She struck me with her palm. Her words wounded more than my stinging cheek. More than the hole in my chest. "Just die." She stumbled back, shivering, bawling, coated with dirt and blood—still beautiful. Still tempting.

"I love you." I approached and guided her shaking hands back to the stake.

"What're you doing?"

"Helping you." The goddess required a sacrifice. Justice demanded it. With my hands over hers, I adjusted the weapon's angle and shoved it deeper, grunting from the impact.

Blood gurgled up my throat and oozed from my chest. One more thrust was needed. It would have to be hers. "Finish it, *cara*."

"Oh, God." She gaped in horror. "What have I done?" She yanked out the spike, then tried to stop the flow.

Tales from the Silver State IV

I swatted her hands and collapsed to my knees. "Don't."

"But you'll die." She swiped my shirt and pressed it to my wound.

"I deserve to."

Her desperate eyes met mine. "I-I don't care."

"*Cosa stai dicendo?* Selene, what are you saying?"

"I don't care," she whispered through silent tears. "I just don't want to be alone anymore."

I LOVE MY PURSE

By Virginia Vennare

I love to shop and Las Vegas is one of the great places to shop in the country. One day while mindlessly wandering through Stein Mart, a small department store in the South West side of town I spotted one of the most unique purses I have ever seen. The darling thing had beige cloth on the outside with little palm trees, monkeys, and a few rhinestones scattered here and there. The lining had blue and white checks and it was all carried about on bamboo, "U" shaped handles. The best part of all was that it was the last one in the store. Maybe I should have said that was **one** of the best parts of buying this purse because, yes it was on sale!

It seemed as though everywhere I went women would notice my purse and say, "What a darling purse, where did you get it?" I would delight in telling them where, then hit them with, "But this was the last one."

Tales from the Silver State IV

The purse went everywhere with me, my Gucci's and Ralph Laren's were left at home in my closet. I didn't care what colors I wore, my purse went with everything.

I went grocery shopping one day at Smith's on Flamingo and Fort Apache and after getting another complement from the check out girl I started to push my cart full of groceries towards my car. My purse was in the child's seat. I opened my trunk and was standing there loading my groceries but when I turned my back to put my groceries in the trunk, I saw something in the corner of my eye. A man had seen my purse in my cart, stopped his car, ran over to where I was standing and I can hardly say it, "grabbed my purse". My heart stopped. I couldn't breathe. I felt a sense of panic coming over me. All I could thing of was **he has my purse**. I didn't think about my credit cards, my check book, my wallet, just my purse.

I watched him as he moved toward his white car with his big ugly hand clutched around the bamboo handles of my bag. A disgusting sight. Without thinking, I grabbed my groceries and started to throw them at him. Jars of pimento stuffed olives, cartons of milk and cans of corn went a flyin. My Italian temper got the best of me and all of my 5'3" 60 year old body went after him. I finally reached him but slipped on the ground and fell inside his car, practically on his lap! He didn't have a chance to close the door yet so there I was, hanging on to the inside running board beside his feet. He looked down at me as though to say "What are you doing you crazy old woman." A look of disbelief and shock was on his face. For a minute I thought, oh my God what if he has a gun or a knife or decided to hit me in the face. Then the realization of what I had done started to sink in. I didn't have a chance to think about it too long because the car slowly started to move forward, dragged me for about a foot then dumped me out onto the blacktop. I was dazed and disoriented; I got up and stood there with shreds of plastic grocery bags still in my hands. My knees were skinned and my elbow was scraped. **He has my purse**. There was an elderly couple in a gray SUV directly behind the cad who just spun off. They stopped briefly to ask me if I was ok and then they started took out after him. Another by-stander offered her cell phone so I could call the police. When I reported it, they said it was already reported by someone who witnessed the incident and were in pursuit. Not too long after that, two police officers showed up. They were very polite, in their starched pressed shirts and their small square walkie talkies attached to their shoulders. One took my report, while the other spoke to another witness. Just a few minutes had passed when the police officer with me started to talk into his shoulder. "Yes, they lost him on Jones Street," "Yes, a white Honda." A few more word exchanges were made, and then before he even finished his report, he said, "They have someone in custody. I'd like you to come with me to try to identify him." I screamed to myself, **he's the guy with the purse with monkies on it you fool.** I got into the police car with the officer. He was asking me to describe my purse and its contents. I did. He was still writing his report, driving, talking into his shoulder and to me, all at the same time. He had only partial control of the steering wheel. I thought I'll be dead before I get a chance to identify this guy.

We arrived at our destination. There were a lot of police cars with their blue and red lights flashing. A white Honda was smashed into a wall. A man in handcuffs was sitting on the curb of the sidewalk. It was him. The police officer asked me if that was the man who grabbed my purse. I'll never for get him, since I looked him right in the eye. I don't often sit in a man's lap without even an introduction. "Yes, that's him."

I was taken across the street & introduced to a detective. He had already taken the purse snatcher's statement. The detective looked about 20 years old, in shorts and a tea shirt with his ID dangling around his neck from a piece of cord. He asked me to sit in his car so he could take my account of what happened. While he got ready we chatted. It was his day off but he heard the chase on his radio and couldn't resist joining in. I thought he must not have much of a life. He told me that taking off after the guy probably wasn't the smartest thing to do but he could understand my reaction.

Tales from the Silver State IV

He asked me why I did it. I told him last time I looked we were still in the United States of America and I believe that people should stand up for what is right. I explained that I was a psychiatric nurse at Montevista Hospital (a behavioral hospital) here in town and was trained to address aggressive behaviors. I acted on instinct. I also believed that people had a right not to be assaulted in their own neighborhoods. Still feel that way. He told me that the car the suspect was driving was stolen and he had an arrest history. The suspect told the police officer that all he wanted was my purse but I surprised him when I came after him like a banchee. I had to give my statement by speaking into a recorder. I was a little nervous, so we had to do it a couple of times because I froze. A lot happened that day.

They took pictures of my bruises and scrapes and then I was taken over to the suspect's car. I was asked to identify the contents of my purse which were scattered all over the back seat of the car. There was a police woman there, taking pictures of my belongings. She retrieved my purse, put it on the top of the car and took a picture of it. Then she said, "What a darling purse, where did you get it?"

www.ingramcontent.com/pod-product-compliance
Lightning Source LLC
Chambersburg PA
CBHW060821120626
46557CB00001B/312